Teruka B Presents...

A Jack Girls'

Love Story

Written By,

Teruka B.

Publisher: Teruka B.

Printed in the USA

ACKNOWLEDGEMENTS

I give all praises to God almighty for giving me this amazing talent and for also giving me the strength even through tough times to be all that I can be.

To my babies Tijah, Karleyah Kevin, Ji'haud thanks so much for always hanging in there with me while I write and lock myself away from the world for hours at a time.

Urban Chapters, you guys are amazing! Jahquel & Saequan, thank you both from the bottom of my heart for everything! I truly appreciate you two!

And last but certainly not least...the readers the love that you guys give me really gives me life. None of this would be possible without you. Hugs and kisses to you all...

This book is dedicated to all my Loyal Supporters for always staying true. I truly appreciate you all more than words could ever express!

Prologue

Where Do I Begin?

I guess, I'll start off by telling you guys that as of right now, we're living in our station wagon. Me my sister and our mother. We had been living here for the past four months, and it's been hell. Especially since we still had to go to school, and act like everything was okay.

Our mother Janelle had been working as a sales representative at a local car dealership, but the owner's son ended up losing it in a poker game gone left. Nevertheless, our mother lost her job and since that was the only job experience that she had over the past twenty years. She was stuck not finding a job that she wanted, and for whatever reason, she refused welfare and unemployment. I don't know I guess it was her pride, but she needed to put that to the side, if you ask me. My sister, and I were only thirteen and fourteen, so we couldn't get a job. Since I was almost fifteen, my mother let me clean for this older lady that she knew. She only paid me twenty dollars a week, which was spent on food.

Although I was young, this lifestyle was degrading to me. I knew that I couldn't do this much longer.

"Eww, Khouri you smell musty as hell!" Bella shouted out while we were at the lunch table, causing everyone to erupt in laughter. Bella Horne was a bratty mixed girl that had never seen a bad day in her life. Nobody liked her for real. She only had friends because she basically bought them. "It smells like you been taking baths in hot dog water, girl!"

Don't get me wrong, she was very pretty, but her personality and attitude made her ugly to me. She just didn't carry herself right at all.

My sister looked at me and closed her eyes. She already knew what type of time I was about to be on. Honestly, I think the only real reason I got so pissed because her boyfriend, Nahmir/Slim the guy I secretly had a crush on was sitting right there. I'm not too sure but I think he knew I did low key, which was why he didn't try to laugh, but I saw him chuckle.

"You dirty ass mush mouth bitch!" I shouted as I stood to my feet and snatched her ass up by the top of her head. She, of course started screaming and kicking. I tried my best to beat her face off before Nahmir pulled me off her ass, after which the principal came rushing over there with security.

I had been suspended multiple times in the past year because of all the stress that I was under at home and school. My mother was gonna probably beat my ass, but I didn't even care at this point.

"What were you thinking, Khouri?" Honestii spat. "Momma is gonna kill you this time.

I knew she was, but I just rolled my eyes at my sister and headed into the principal's office to accept my punishment.

"I can't say that I'm surprised, Khouri. I don't know what has happened with you. Your grades have been dropping, and you're in and out of trouble all the time. What am I gonna do with you?"

I just looked him with no care in the world as I popped my gum. "Yeah, ion know what's wrong with me," I sarcastically replied.

"See, it's this kind of attitude that makes me wonder. You used to be one of my best students. Lately, I just don't know what to think," he spoke.

"Mr. Claytor, can you just tell me what you're doing to punish me? I really don't feel like waiting around in here all day listening to how I used to be," I huffed.

I could tell he was becoming annoyed with my antics when he removed his glasses from his fat face and slowly slung them across his desk.

"You know what? I'm gonna set up a parent teacher conference with your mother because this is going nowhere. For now, you're suspended for ten days. Leave my office. Sit in the lobby and I will call your mother to come get you," he grunted dismissing me.

With no problem, I got my ass up from the hard ass folding chair that sat in his office. When I got out front, and my sister was sitting there with her head hung low. The box braids that she wore dangled on the nasty floor.

"Get 'ya ass up," I told her with a slight giggle.

She looked up and cocked her head and rolled her eyes at me, as she sighed heavily.

"What's the matter?" I huffed.

"Nothing, bruh," she dryly replied.

I sat down not caring what was wrong with her whiny ass.

"Are you serious, Khouri?"

"What the fuck is that supposed to mean?"

"Ugh, it means, we are already going through enough and now this. Ma is gonna flip!"

"Girl, bye with allat! That bitch shouldn't have been running her dick suckers! Period!" I shouted causing everybody in the office to stop what they were doing to look in our direction.

"No, you got mad because you saw that, Slim heard her ass and was laughing."

She was right though. That was the reason I got so livid, and amped on her ass. The fuck she thought! She wasn't about to do that in front of my future nigga.

"Man, whatever! Like I said, she shouldn't have tried me!" I snapped.

Soon as she was about to say something, in walks our mother with her winter coat on, looking raggedy as fuck!

"What the fuck, Khouri Nashe!" She yelled as she yoked me up by the collar of my pink tank top.

"Ma! You're buggin' bruh! She called me out! If it's anybody's fault...it's yours! This shit is embarrassing as hell!" I yelled out as I stepped away from her. I just knew she was about to plug my ass. Instead she dragged me out behind her.

"Bring y'all ass on here!"

After we got away from the school, she pulled the wagon over at a Great Stops on East Market Street, down from A & T University. My sister and I looked at each other completely confused.

She turned the car off once she got a parking spot and turned to us.

"Listen girls, I get it. I really do, but y'all can't fold right now! I'm about to show y'all how to get this bread!" She grilled.

I loved my mother, but shorty was on some other shit!

"Khouri, you're supposed to be making a better example, and the shit you're doing is ridiculous! I've been holding out on y'all! I mean, I can't keep allowing you girls to think shit is sweet when it's not!"

As she yapped her jaws, I was off in wonderland thinking about my nigga...Slim. Well, his real name was, Nahmir Lamar Christian. Yeah, I know. That nigga name was fucked up, but I loved his ass...

"What do you mean ma?" Honestii quizzed in confusion.

"You about to find out," my mother retorted as she started the engine again.

Honestii looked over to me with a raised brow. In return, I just shrugged my shoulders.

"Where are we going?" I dryly asked.

"I'm taking y'all to the Four Seasons baby. I'm gonna show you girls how to boost. It's simple. All you gotta do is follow my lead. Once we get everything. Then we'll bounce and take it to the hood and sell it for half or a third of the retail price," she explained.

"Wait...so you're taking us, your daughters to go steal?" I spat.

"Let's just call it borrowing," she replied with a slight chuckle.

"Momma, I don't feel comfortable doing this," Khouri huffed.

"Right! What if we get caught or something? Ugh, just get a job!"

As soon as the words rolled off my tongue, I regretted it. I just knew that was my ass. That was one thing my mother didn't tolerate, and that was us being disrespectful to her in any fashion. After a few moments of silence, our mother spoke.

"You know what? Today I'm gonna give your ass a pass, Khouri. But don't you ever part your fuckin' lips to talk to me like that!"

"I'm sorry, but do we have to do this?" I replied.

"Yes, you do! This is gonna help us make extra money. Until we get on our feet, this is what is about to happen, and I don't wanna hear shit else about it!"

That was it, and we couldn't do shit about it. My sister and I just sat there pouting until we got to the mall.

Once our mother parked in front of Dickey's and hopped slam out the car leaving us with no choice but to follow her.

Looking at each other I reluctantly got out the car and my sister followed suit.

Upon entering the mall, we headed straight to DTLR. We looked around for a little while as our mother had a salesclerk to help her. After trying on several pair of shoes, the salesclerk became annoyed and went to help other people. That's when our mother slipped her shoes off and put the new all-red, Nike Huarache shoes and started walking out the store.

Grabbing my sister by the arm, I drug her out the store fast as I could. I was scared as shit. My palms were sweating, and my heart nearly jumped out my chest.

Our mother didn't even touch on the fact that she had just stole the shoes, she just entered Forever 21 like it was nothing.

She grabbed a couple of items and stuffed them into her pants and looked at us signaling us to do the same. We looked around and did as she had done, and fast walked out the store.

I'm not gonna lie, when she first told us what we had to do. I was highly disappointed in her, but that adrenaline rush that I got from stealing was amazing. I had never in my life been so scared and excited all at once.

From that very day my sister and I became the slickest thieves in the city...

Khouri

Well, I'm eighteen now, and shit was just the same. We were still boosting clothes and whatever else we could get our hands on, just to make money. Thankfully we were now in our own place, so it wasn't as badly as it was before. Nevertheless, we still had a damn curfew because momma wasn't having it.

Honestii was about to be seventeen, so I didn't see the logic in our mother's rules, but we didn't question them. We just abided by them. She said long as we were under her roof, we would have a curfew. After all she was the reason for us getting out of that damn car.

The house we lived in before going homeless, our mother was able to get it back. The neighborhood was trash as fuck, but at least now we had a place to stay. I just couldn't wait for us to get a house in a better area.

Honestii and I had moved on to bigger shit! There was no way we were gonna go back to sleeping in the damn car. Our mother had landed a job as an assistant manager at a major car dealership, so she was holding the rent and bills down, so we were straight. The money we made, was for play-play...

Our mother knew that we were still doing dumb shit, but she didn't care. As far as her knowing everything that we had going on. She had no idea.

"Come on, hurry up before that nigga wakes up," I rushed my sister before leaving out the door of our latest victim's home. That's right, we were even jacking these niggas for their bread.

When I got out to the car, I noticed that Honestii wasn't with me. I immediately snatched my cell out my bra and dialed her; only because I knew she had her phone on vibrate.

I swear Honestii was always taking forever to do anything. I loved my sister to death, but she was too damn slow. If I didn't know any better, I would have sworn that she didn't like getting the fast money anymore. I just prayed that I was wrong because I needed her by my side.

"Bitch! Hurry the fuck up! What is taking you so damn long?" I shouted into the phone.

She didn't utter a word. Just as I was about to get out of the car and personally hurry her ass along, she came out skipping towards the damn car. I watched closely as I slid the gear in *'drive'* and prayed that Premo, the nigga we had just robbed wasn't coming out behind her careless ass.

"Damn did it take you long enough?" I huffed as I mashed off without letting her close the car door.

"Whatever, I had to do that shit right because I'm tired of you always having something to say about leaving evidence, so shut that shit the hell up!" She spat.

I couldn't front my sister was right. I did always have a problem about her ass and the way she was jacking niggas. Like I said, it was like she didn't really want to do it anymore being all careless and shit.

Shaking the disturbing thoughts, I pulled up to our crib and parked before we separated the money. The total was three thousand eight hundred and seventy-five dollars. I made three piles. I put mine in my bra, handed my sister hers plus took extra pile so that she could take our mother her cut.

Even though she didn't know much about how we were getting money, she still demanded her cut.

"Ahem, you not coming in?" she huffed putting her hands on her hips.

"Nah," I replied answering with a sneaky grin. "I'll be back shortly."

She knew I had other plans on how I was going to spend my night, but I didn't tell my mother though. I wasn't stupid. She probably assumed that I was going to Nahmir's spot and she would be right.

"Alright heffa, be careful and don't do nothing I wouldn't do," Honestii teased as she eased up out of the ride.

I always tried to make sure that she knew where I was going no matter what the situation was. There were some crazy ass people in the world. One thing about it though. I could be crazier!

"Did you hear me KK?" My sister spoke a little louder. "Be careful!"

"I will and please don't tell ma'," I pleaded. I passed her an extra twenty-dollar bill, just so she would be less likely to tell on my ass.

No matter how old I got, my mother always scared the shit out of me, and I refused to get my ass beat at eighteen.

"Oh, shut that shit up, you know I gotcha," Honestii assured sashaying off. "I love you KK!"

"I love you too!" I yelled driving off.

The lifestyle we were living was something more than I ever thought it would be. Not only did we have a new crib, but we had cash on hand all the time.

Honestly, when we started boosting I never in a million years would have thought it would have gotten this far. I mean at the time it was a survival of the fittest situation, and now it was for the enjoyment. Now I'm addicted to this shit. I got an adrenaline rush every time I took what didn't belong to me.

'Hell, who wouldn't? It was fucking free to me!'

As I let those memories simmer to the back of my mind, I pulled up to my bae's secret lair. I parked in the crowded rocky lot that sat adjacent to his large two-story spot.

I took my J's off and slid on my red bottoms when I parked. Soon as I got out, I prepared to step across the uneven ground and tried my best not to fall and bust my ass in the heels. "Shit," I complained once I made it to the door and damn near tripped.

I hurried to catch myself by grabbing the handle before I fell. Thank goodness because when I turned around there was some fine ass nigga coming up right behind my ass.

"You aight boo?" He asked as he gently wrapped his arm around my waist and opened the door for me.

"Yeah, thanks," I stuttered and took my ass in and went to the downstairs bar before my man caught my ass flirting.

It was pumping as usual. Nahmir always had niggas and bitches in and out of his second crib on weekends. This was one of his many hustles' and he did it well. Yes, he had a crib on the other side of town that I would stay at from time to time. Of course, I would always have to act like I was staying at my girl, Dutchess crib though.

Nahmir was twenty years old and a big-time gambler. The nigga was addicted to it and I fell right into the lifestyle with him. He hosted parties at this house he owned and fixed up into a little hot spot. Everyone that wanted to participate had to pay a hundred-dollar entrance fee. So, every night he made a minimum of five thousand on the door alone.

When I first met him in school, he was with that raggedy ass heffa, Bella. I showed her ass though. She thought making fun of me that day in the lunchroom was gonna stop me, but it only made me go at him that much harder. I still ended up getting her man.

After that incident my mother changed our schools, so that I wouldn't get into trouble anymore, but I was still angry because of our situation, so I used any excuse not to go to school. I hated Grimsley High School and everyone in it, so did my sister. We were constantly in trouble.

One day, my sister and I was at the mall boosting out of Victoria Secrets and he saw me. I swear I thought I was gonna lose my shit right there, but when my eyes met his, I didn't care what he was saying to be honest. He was so damn fine that he had me at, '*hey shorty*'.

We talked for a few, and I put my shit all the way out there. I figured what did I have to lose. Surprisingly he sympathized with me, and he put me on to his spot. That was where I was making my secret side money. If I wasn't running the blackjack table, I was running niggas pockets. That was one of the reasons why I kept going back.

Of course, the other reason was his ass. I was extremely attracted to him and hell I had always been in love with him. At first, he tried to act like he was just trying to be a good friend, but not long after that he was claiming what was rightfully his baby, and Bella's ass was history! Yes, they were still together after high school and everything.

After I got a tipsy, I began my search for my man, which I found him pretty much right away.

"What's up baby," Nahmir greeted as I walked upstairs into the *'smoke room'* and found him in a secluded corner wrapping up a phone call and putting out his blunt.

"Nothing just dropped my sister off." I smiled. "What's up with you?"

"You baby," he flirted. "So, are you ready to get this money wit' ya boy tonight or what?"

"You know that's all I got on my mind," I clarified as I went in for a kiss.

Although I had mad love for Nahmir, for some reason, I just didn't trust that ass. He swore up and down that I was the only bitch he was fucking around with, but I knew better.

'Let me tell y'all why...'

In the beginning of the relationship Nahmir was putting it down daily, but lately it was barely three times a week. That was what raised the red flag in the first place. Something was up 'wit that nigga, I just couldn't put my finger on it though, so I played my position. That was one thing I had learned during this journey was to keep my mouth shut until I found out what I needed to know.

Don't get me wrong, he didn't have bitches calling his phone or stopping by his crib or the gambling spot on some mad shit. He was smarter than that, but I was even smarter and just waiting for the chance to catch him slipping. Like I said, shit was different.

I knew if his ass was knocking another bitch off, it would come to the light sooner or later. All I had to do was keep my eyes open. The streets talked; and so, does the jealous bitches...

One thing about a side bitch, they get hurt and want to make sure the main girl finds out about the affair. They do that shit in hopes of fucking up their home lives. What they don't realize in the process is that nine times out of ten that shit don't work, and they end up losing the sorry ass nigga anyway, at the least. Plus, these hoes didn't want no smoke with the kid...

Dumb bitches liked to learn the hard way. Not me, I was taught very well by watching my mother and the no-good ass men she laid up with. They lied better than rugs and Nahmir was starting to prove that he was no different. He felt like just because he was a few years older than I was he could pull shit over on me. He considered me still *'green'*, but a bitch was far from that.

Just like he thought he was talking me out of my goodies, when all the while I was getting just what I wanted. He played right into my hand.

With sex on the brain, I allowed Nahmir to kiss my lips passionately as he caressed my ass. He was heating me up to the point where I was ready to ride the dick, but soon as I got ready to make my move his ass pulled back.

"Come on let's go downstairs where everybody at," he said clinching my hand while ushering me towards the stairs.

I rolled my eyes and followed behind him. Soon as we got down to the basement, he dropped my hand quick, fast and in a hurry. I ignored his arrogant ass and tossed my jacket on the love sofa before I headed back to the bar. He was seriously working my nerves.

While at the bar, the same fine ass dude from outside came up to me trying to flirt. "Hey beautiful, can I buy you a drink?"

"Nah thanks. I'm good. I can buy my own drinks love," I winked.

Extending his hand, he introduced himself as Kanen. The way he was all up in my grill, I took it as he didn't know that I was Nahmir's girl.

As I lifted my head up to look him in the face, I could tell he was feeling it. The last thing I needed was a drunk in my face. I could tell his ass had money too, so his ass had to get *'got'.*

"Hey baby," he slurred as he spun around towards me eyeing me down hungrily. "You sho' look good as fuck!"

Kanen put his arms around me and tried to caress my boob with his free hand. As badly as I wanted to knee him in the nuts and spit in his face, I didn't. Instead I took the opportunity to run his damn pockets.

First, I looked around to make sure no one was checking for me, I eased up out my seat and stood between his legs. I wrapped my arms around his waist, making sure to move as much as I could. When I brought them out, I had completely stripped Kanen for every bill he had on him.

'Fuckin' dummy!'

Soon as I was finished, I backed up off him. Honestly, I wanted him as far away from me as possible.

"I'm gonna need you to get up off of me before my nigga, Nahmir comes out here and see you all up on me like this," I huffed slightly shoving him up off me. I thought I was gonna throw up in my damn mouth when I saw his little baby dick poking out when I broke away. I couldn't do shit but laugh.

"Oh shit, you Slim's girl?" He asked holding his hands high up in the air. "Yo, my bad man. Please don't tell that nigga!" He begged.

I just smirked and got my ass away from him. I swear I wasn't even three steps away from his ass before another thirsty bitch was all up on him. That was just what I needed to throw the sent off me once Kanen found himself robbed.

Taking my ass directly to the bathroom, I counted what I had gotten off Kanen. "Damn!" I had six hundred and eighty-seven dollars. That shit made my pussy jump because not even Nahmir knew I had that extra bread. That meant no cut for his ass tonight.

You see we usually split whatever I made while I was up in his spot. But sometimes I had to look out for my damn self, and this was one of those times...

After stashing my extra cash, I freshened up my MAC gloss and brushed my hair. I couldn't help but stare at my reflection before leaving out of the bathroom. I was growing up way too damn fast, but I did look good.

I headed back out into the midst of the action, and surprisingly that shit was still jumping.

Since Nahmir had his aunt Falita working the blackjack table, I didn't have to do shit but mingle and snatch pockets. By the end of the night, after giving my man his cut, my ass was two-grand richer.

"Now this is what the fuck I'm talkin' 'bout," I whispered to myself before joining Nahmir in the front.

It was time to close and the workers were putting the chairs up on the tables so that they could clean the floors. The second we were done this nigga started the fucking interrogation.

"So how much money did you snatch from that nigga Kanen?"

"What? You're trippin' I didn't get shit from that nigga," I lied. "I wish I would have though because tonight's take would have been lovely."

"Come on now Khouri, I taught you the game. Don't try to run that shit right back on me," he warned. "You don't think I see everything up in my own shit?"

I stood there for a few minutes fumbling with my phone looking around aimlessly and shit before I spoke up.

"Alright bruh, damn! I got about six," I huffed with irritation.

"See that's all you had to do was keep it real with me girl."

"Man, the white man is about to turn off my mama's lights," I lied. "That's the only reason I didn't include that in with the other bread."

I knew I had to think quick on my feet, and I really didn't like lying like that, but I needed to use it to my advantage at moment. I wanted a new Michael Kors bag and I didn't want to break bank to do it. That shit wasn't about to happen.

"Don't worry about it baby you can keep my cut on the six. Next time, just come to me so that I can take care of the bill for you," he insisted with a smile. "You know if you need any help at home I gotcha shorty, remember that okay?"

"I will but look baby I gotta go. I'm gonna try to sneak out later and come over, but I can't make any promises. You know my mom be on some other shit."

"Okay well call me first because a nigga is tired than a muthafucka baby," Nahmir suggested before kissing me deeply.

"Alright baby," I told him leaving his ass at the door.

See that was why I had trust issues with that nigga because it was always that, *'Call me before you come'* shit. I was going to surprise his ass one night and go over there without calling. He had me fucked up.

'I wish I would catch him with a bitch!'

It's cool though because I knew that muthafucka was up to some sneaky shit. I didn't know what though.

I wasn't about to chase his ass to find out either. Instead, I decided to let his stupid ass hang himself...

Honestii

My sister was taking all night to come home, and I didn't know how much longer I could cover for her ass. Our mother was questioning the hell out of me and I was running out of valid excuses. I stood in the front window hoping to see her ass pull up, but I swear the more I looked the longer it took her ass to get there.

My heart dropped when I heard our mothers' bedroom door squeak as she opened it. "Fuck," I sighed heavily. "I already knew she was about to spaz."

"Where the fuck is your sister at? And I know she told 'ya ass so don't lie, dammit!"

"I don't know where she is ma," I lied.

"You better not be fuckin' lying to me either, Honestii!"

Ugh! She was really blowing me. I knew this shit was gonna happen if she took too damn long! Khouri was always irresponsible, but damn. I walked back in my room to try and avoid our mother, but she was still talking shit.

"If she's out calling herself makin' money 'ya ass had better tell me right now!" She demanded as she barged into my room. "I don't want her out there all alone with no one to watch her damn back! I know she better not be with that no-good ass nigga, Nahmir/Slim or whatever y'all call his ugly ass!"

Momma was old school and knew all about Nahmir and his hustle. It was something that ran in his family and she didn't trust his ass one bit, especially when it came to Khouri.

"She just barely turned eighteen and I know his ass is every bit of twenty-three, if not older!"

"Mom, why are you yelling at me?" I huffed. "I don't know where she is."

"Because I want to know where the fuck your sister is, that's why the hell I'm yelling!"

"For real mom?" I yawned and wiped my eyes hoping that she would leave again and shut the door. That shit didn't happen. She was really starting to get on my damn nerves.

"If I dial her phone one more time and she..."

"Here she comes now!" I interrupted as I heard Khouri come through the front door and slam it. Momma was yelling too much for her to have heard anything.

Soon as my mother stepped foot out of my room to let my sister have it, I jumped up and closed the door behind her. I turned my lights off then hurried my ass right under my blankets. I didn't have time for the bullshit. She had been talking enough shit and I didn't wanna hear anymore.

They yelled for the longest and I stayed in my lane. Putting my headphones in my ears, I didn't remove the covers until the sun came up the next morning. Making it Saturday and I was ready to get into something.

Hurrying to my stash, I went and counted how much money I had saved. I sat there thumbing through hundred after hundred until I reached the sum of a hefty six-thousand, seven hundred and eighty dollars. I peeled off the seven-eighty, threw it onto the bed. I put the rest back into my lockbox and placed it back where I had it stashed.

At seventeen years old that was a whole lot of money to me and I knew my mother and sister would think the same. That was why I hid the shit from them too. Yes, I usually told my sister everything, but in this case, I couldn't risk her telling mom when she got mad. I loved my mother to death, but I wasn't trying to give her my fucking bread either. That was our mothers' downfall. She was money hungry. I guess you can say that was something she and my sister has in common.

"What the hell are you doing?" Khouri yelled through the door. "Why you always gotta lock your door?"

"Did you ever think that I want some damn privacy sometime?" I smacked my lips and went to crack the door wide enough for her to see my face. "What's up?"

My sister wasn't going for it. She barged in my room; something she had always done. That shit was so annoying.

Once inside, Khouri's eyes shifted from mine to the money on my bed. Her nosy ass couldn't resist.

"Where the hell are you going?" She quizzed.

"To the mall," I smirked as I got my clothes ready to go and shower. "You need to come with me too."

"I thought you were saving your money Mrs. Lil' Goodie," she replied jokingly. "And hell nah, I ain't trying to spend my coins just yet."

"I am, saving so hush the fuck up," I laughed. "You wanna go? I'll buy you something." I knew that would get her attention.

"Even that Tiffany bracelet that I have been dying to get?" Khouri probed.

"How much is it?" I asked giving her a serious side eye.

"Only a one-eighty," she giggled giving me her innocent grin. Of course, I laughed. She is my sister and we are thick as fuck! I know what her next move is, and she knows mine.

"Aight sis. I gotcha," I agreed. "Go get ready. The bus comes in a few."

"The bus? Ain't nobody riding that shit!" she snapped.

"Yeah, you know after last night mom ain't gonna let you drive her damn car!"

"Watch and see," Khouri plotted as she rushed out my room and closed the door.

Not even five minutes later she returned dangling the keys in my face. I should have known she would get her way. Mom always spoiled the hell out of her ass, and I was the damn baby. I didn't understand it for the life of me.

Within the next hour Khouri and I were on our way to the mall. While I was watching the road, her ass was calling and texting Nahmir's ass.

"Put that damn phone down and watch the road!" I fussed. "Ain't nobody trying to die over some dick!"

"Where the fuck he at?" She pouted as she got out of the car in the crowded mall parking lot and slammed the door. She had completely ignored my request. The bitch ignored me altogether.

"He's probably sleeping or in the bathroom, dang, stop sweating him," I teased.

"Just come on and let's go in Tiffany's before you start spending on ya bankroll."

"Shut the hell up, Khouri because I know ya ass got a pocket full of money too! 'Ya ass lucky I'm being nice."

Khouri didn't say a word. She just led me into the jeweler's and picked out her gift.

Once we were done, we went out to locate the nearest shoe store. I was dying for a new pair of J's.

"Thank you, sister," she smiled genuinely as I placed her bracelet on her wrist for her. She then hugged me, pulled away then gasped. "Dang, I think I left my cell on the counter inside of the store."

Before I could respond, Khouri had dashed back into Tiffany's and left me standing there looking crazy. I didn't want to linger like I was about to steal some shit, so I went over to a nearby bench and took a seat.

Soon as I sat down, I heard a familiar voice.

"Baby you know what's up," he spoke seductively.

Squinting my eyes, I slowly turned around, and I saw Nahmir's dog ass. He was strolling right by me with his arm around some high yellow chick. When I got a closer look, I recognized that it was Bella's ass! Yes, his ex-shorty from high school. He was so busy up in her face that he didn't even notice me.

'Oh, this nigga bold as fuck!'

I couldn't hop my ass up fast enough to go find my sister. She had to see the shit for herself. That wasn't something I could just tell her. I know she is gonna fucking flip.

"Hey!" Khouri greeted me at the entrance with a bag. "Sorry baby."

When she handed it to me, I took it and gave her a confused look. "What's this?"

"Just open it."

After giving her another funny expression, I dug my hand down into the bag and retrieved a small box. When I opened it, I found a gold bracelet inside with a *'Sisters'* pendant hanging off.

When I looked up to thank Khouri, she held up her wrist to show me that she had the very same one on her opposite arm. "Sisters for life, baby!" She chanted.

We began to hug tightly and when we released, I remembered about seeing Nahmir. Just that quickly I had forgot. I immediately scanned the perimeter to see if he was still in sight.

"Who are you looking for?"

"No one," I lied. "I thought I saw mom's friend that we hit last week.

"Are you serious?" She whispered ducking. "Let's get the hell out of here then."

That shit ended my shopping spree and I hadn't even bought anything for myself yet...

I was livid because that was the whole point of the damn trip. But there was no way I was gonna let her run into Nahmir's ass, especially seeing that he wasn't only cheating, but with the very bitch that Khouri thought she had taken him from.

Khouri tried calling him, but she still couldn't get an answer.

****

Of course, later that night, I ended up telling Khouri about seeing him at the mall with the bitch Bella Horne. Just like I expected, my sister hopped right on the phone to confront him. I swear if this was a cartoon, I would be able to see smoke coming from her ears. I knew she wouldn't let me know, but I could tell that she was hella hurt.

I assumed that Khouri didn't get the answers she wanted so she hung up and shoved her cell in her pocket.

"Change of plans bitch! Fuck his funny looking ass! He gonna make me fuck him up!"

"What you mean?"

"We're not going to Slim's bullshit spot tonight. We're gonna go to this new spot that opened last week. Everyone is gonna be there too!"

"You gonna run that shit by ma, right?" I quizzed. "She already gonna be on bullshit because 'ya ass fucked up last night."

"On my way now," She smiled heading to our mothers' room. "You know she gonna let us go because her greedy ass is gonna want a cut anyway."

Once again, she came back with a wide grin spread across her face. Yes, she talked mom into letting us go to Mr. D's just that fast.

Mr. D's is a club that was for teens and shit under twenty-one. What she didn't know was that you had to be eighteen to get in. Lucky for us Khouri got the hookup.

We got dressed and headed to the spot. "Damn, it's packed up in here!"

My sister started complaining soon as we got there. It never failed. She was ready to cuss out anyone that got in her way. I felt sorry for whoever that was going to be that night...

"What's that?" I questioned after I saw her shove a small flask down into her purse. "I know that ain't no fucking alcohol?"

"Don't worry about this right here," she snapped. "I ain't gonna get fucked up to the point where I can't drive, and if I do, you got a Learner's Permit. I know you don't like to, but you can drive my ass around."

Ignoring her totally, I trailed right behind her into the club and found myself a table. I was already feeling drained.

"You just gonna sit over here or are you gonna get up and mingle?" Khouri asked slapping my arm

"Mingle with who girl?"

"All these fine ass niggas up in here," Khouri smirked putting her hands out. "You ain't never gonna get a man sitting on your ass."

"Number one, I can't get no money up in here. It ain't nothing but a bunch of broke ass boys!" I huffed stepping out of my element. "Number two, show me one fine dude and I'll step to him."

My sister grabbed her mouth and widened her eyes. She was making a big deal out of my response and her ass was about to run with it. She was so damn extra, I swear. I couldn't do shit but laugh at her antics.

"Okay," she hummed scanning the club. "Him right there."

"Too short."

"Okay, that one right there," she pointed.

"Hell nah, he needs to cut his damn hair!"

"You're being picky tonight, huh?" she laughed taking her time to find the next one. "Okay look Sis. Him right there. He's coming towards us now. I'm about to go over here she said walking over by the restrooms. I can't wait to see what you got."

Before I had the opportunity to object, Khouri got up from the table and eased over to the beverage counter. I watched her and as soon as we gained eye contact, I winked.

Meanwhile the guy in the brown sweater, light blue jeans and Timbs was moving closer and closer. I had to wait for the right moment. I had a plan. Well, I think I have a good enough plan.

"Oh, excuse me," I smiled as I stood up just as he came close enough so that I could bump into him a bit.

"Oh, no," he grinned. "That was my fault ma'."

Backing up just a little, I continued locking eyes with the handsome stranger, and before I knew it, he was asking for my name. "It's Honestii," I seductively replied.

"Well, Honestii, is it? You look a little young to be up in here."

"Why thank you," I flirted trying to act as mature as I could. "Don't worry. I'm old enough to be wherever I wanna be." Of course, I lied.

"So, what's up? You still in school?" He probed.

I laughed it off, but this nigga was a little bit too nosey for my taste.

"Yeah, I'm a senior at Grimsley High," I replied with a tight grin.

I graduated from Dudley a couple of years ago."

"You did ah, ah..."

"Oh, my bad beautiful, my name is Marlon."

"Okay. Well, it's nice to meet you Marlon," I blushed.

Unexpectedly, he took my hand into his. "It's nice to meet you also, Honestii. I like your name by the way. It says a lot about you."

"Why, thank you."

Well, to say the least, I hushed up my sisters' big ass mouth, but she still managed to come by the table and introduce herself as well. Yes, she embarrassed me…

"Damn, y'all look just alike. Y'all twins or some shit?" he asked.

"No, we are eleven months apart though," I answered honestly. "It's just us two so we are really close."

After Khouri's ass finally left us alone, Marlon started telling me about himself. He explained how he was into Marketing and Sales. He was already a manager at his office and was making good money. His resume was very impressive, to say the least.

Once he finished briefly filling me in on his background, he asked about me. I told him what I felt comfortable sharing and before I knew it the lights were coming on. It was midnight, which indicated closing time.

I hated that I had lied to him about being older than what I was, because I could clearly tell that he had to be in his mid-twenties. *'Who knows, we may never speak again,'* I thought.

My heart jumped immediately. We had missed our curfew.

"What's wrong?" Marlon inquired after he saw me spring to my feet.

"I just need to find my sister," I told him peering around the room.

"She's over there talking to the owner," he informed me as he pointed towards the front of the club. "I think she's waving you down."

Marlon asked for my number and we quickly exchanged, then I rushed my ass over to Khouri. She was smiling, but I didn't understand why until we got in the car.

"Bitch! Why are you grinning and we're late for curfew? You may not care about mom going the fuck off on us, but I do! I don't want to hear the shit!" I huffed as we headed back to the house.

"Here 'Lil whining ass girl," Khouri laughed as she threw two hundred dollars in my lap. "If that fine ass nigga you were talking to, didn't make it worth getting in trouble, maybe this will."

Our mother was sitting in front of the door when we got home. I just knew she was about to fuck us up too, but all she did was hold her fuckin' hand out for some money.

Me and my sister looked at each other in utter disgust, I shut the hell up as I watched my sister pull off two-hundred dollars and pass it to her.

Afterwards I went and locked myself in my room so that I could add the money to my stash.

No sooner than I got in my PJ's, Khouri was peeking her head in my door.

"Can you believe your fuckin' momma," she whispered.

"Naw, that is your momma. She be doing the most. How is she gonna be sitting at the fuckin' door with the audacity to have her damn hand out," I huffed.

"You know she money hungry as fuck! I just overlook her anymore," Khouri replied.

"That's fine and dandy, but what if we didn't get shit tonight! She acts like we couldn't just go have a good time without trying to scam a nigga."

"You know I already know. I love her dearly, but she gets on my damn nerves too. Don't worry, we about to start moving different. I love you sis."

"I love you too."

It may have been worth it, but I couldn't wait to get the hell out of mom's spot. I wasn't with the rules and regulations, but I was going to abide by them long as I was under her roof. I did have that much sense...

Khouri

Exactly one week after Honestii graduated, she and I got our own spot at Tyler Village. It was a pleasant little sub-division right outside of the city. Our mother finally moved out of that little ratty ass neighborhood and got her a little spot about twenty-minutes away from us. She decided to rent to property out since it was now paid in full.

Once we moved out, I copped a nice whip. Right after, since Honestii finally got her Driver's License, she got a car as well. Trust me, she didn't want to, but I wasn't having it. She kept asking to use mine but as soon as I told her *'no'*, she rushed her ass out and got one but still barely drove it. She was a cheap ass.

I mean this little heffa was so damn tight with her money that she would even catch the bus places on nice days just so she wouldn't have to get gas. She was always finding a way to save a damn dime. I couldn't understand it. We were getting money every other day. It wasn't like she didn't have money to spare. That shit must have come from our no-good ass daddy side of the family, because I was money hungry like my mother, ugh that was hard to admit. Now I need to wash my mouth out.

Yes, although we moved out of our mother's crib, she still hooked us up with marks. Only now we didn't have to give her as much money as before. She had a side hustle of her own popping off.

As for my personal life, I was still fucking with Nahmir on the money tip. Our relationship wasn't like it was before because that dirty muthafucka cheated on me with that nasty ass bitch Bella Horne. I still couldn't believe how he had the audacity to ever be out with her ass in public while we were exclusive...or so I thought. That was a few months ago now. I hadn't let him tap this ass since. My feelings were beyond hurt, and he had been doing everything he could to make it up to me. To make things worse, it was hard as hell not to give him my goodies, but I had to show him. He couldn't do me just any old kind of way. His ass would not only take accountability, but I had to be sure that his heart was in it like mine was.

Nahmir didn't have a clue how sprung I was. My sister didn't even know. I kept it on the inside while on the outside I acted tough as a nail.

It didn't matter how many times Nahmir tried to convince me that he would never step outside of the relationship again, I hardly believed that ass. I didn't trust him as far as I could throw him, and he was a thick ass nigga.

"I need that one faithful nigga on my team," I huffed.

That was exactly what I needed and Nahmir still hadn't proven to me that he was the one. He hadn't been doing shit but supporting my hustle and fucking me when I needed it, and now that the fucking wasn't happening. I was starting to wonder what I even needed him for.

Other than that, he and I had been keeping it cordial. I had to do shit like that to hold him back at a distance. If I didn't, I would grow weak and give into him every time.

"Damn," I yelled out as my sister busted through my bedroom door ripping me from my silent rant.

"What's up Sis?" Honestii sang happily as she pranced her ass all up in my room without knocking, as usual. I guess I couldn't complain. I did the same thing to her ass.

"Damn, I ain't even gonna say shit," I smirked as I laid back onto my bed and closed my eyes.

"Where's Slim? It's Saturday night and y'all ain't out scheming? This is new," she teased.

"I would ask you the same thing, but we all know how Marlon is," I said jokingly, laughing at myself.

Even though the men in our lives supported our independence, Marlon wanted Honestii to get a regular job, and be like his ass. He didn't want her to keep taking the risks, rather that was the excuse he gave her. Nigga claimed he was worried about her ending up in jail or dead.

Now Nahmir, was just the exact opposite. He wanted me to stay on my grind. In fact, he kept introducing me to different hustles. He was about his paper and so was I. That's what made us such a good team... I guess. The only thing that was missing was trust, respect, loyalty, and communication. To me that is what made a great relationship. See, I'm not big on all that other shit. Honestly that's what was keeping us from being more.

To be honest, I loved Slim with all my heart and he was the only man I wanted to be with. I just couldn't play that hand right now. Lord knows telling his ass that I love him was off the table. I had to wait until he revealed his hand and told me first. Don't get me wrong, we always said it before, but now to my heart it was gonna be fake, which is why I didn't tell him.

"Well alright," Honestii yelled then waved knocking me right up out of my trance once again. I couldn't get right for shit. "Marlon and I are going out to dinner. You want me to bring you something back?"

"No, I'm good. Thanks Sis and y'all be careful," I replied as I climbed beneath my covers. "Hit that light on your way out."

Soon as my sister was gone out of my room, I began drifting off with a light snore. Now usually I would wake up, but the thought of Nahmir was on my mind. I couldn't interrupt that now, could I...

****

A few weeks passed and I still hadn't gotten any closer to getting a commitment from Nahmir. The only thing I could do was throw myself into my work.

'RING, RING'

My cell rang causing me to jump up quickly. Looking down at the screen I saw that it was my mother. She was calling for me and Honestii to come over to our old house on the south side to lick some nigga she had just met named Big Bob. We still owned it and rented it out but during the time we were in between tenants, so mom hooked it up for us to use when the perfect victim slid through.

"Are you for real?" I asked dreading to go back to our old neighborhood. I hated it there.

"Yes, now listen to this…" my mother began to briefly put me up to speed on Big Bob's background.

She said that word on the street was that Big Bob was a big-time hustler that kept a pocket full of money with his old ass. My mother told me all about how he got down, so I was a little leery about doing it. I didn't know if the risk was worth the reward.

"Come on now KK, this is a for sure thing. I already got it set up. He's gonna stop by here right after his pickup. He's gonna be holding a helluva bag too."

I really didn't want to do it, but I agreed to it anyway. That was our mother, and I hated to let her down.

The next thing I had to do was get my sister on board and just like I expected, she didn't want to do it either. I swear it took like an hour to convince her ass to come along for the ride. I swear I don't think I had heard her talk so much shit in my life.

"You know we ain't got to do this right?" My sister huffed as we climbed into the car to leave. "I supposed to out having dinner with my nigga, but you and ya damn momma working my nerves! I have a bad feeling about this shit!"

"Bitch if you don't stop with that lovey dovey shit...," I teased.

"You should try it! You always want to act so fucking hard..."

"Hush that shit up Honestii! I need to concentrate on the shit we about to do! You fuckin' my head up with all that noise!" I snapped as I gripped the steering wheel and took a deep breath.

She took heed and left me the hell alone. She didn't say another word for the duration of the trip.

"Let's just go in here, do this shit and get the hell out, aight?" I told her.

I looked around and couldn't believe how badly the neighborhood changed so much in such a short time. I mean it was the hood when we lived there, but this whole shit looked like a street full of trap houses. It was sad because this is where I spent my first ten years on earth. Of course, when our dead-beat ass daddy left us, we had to sell and move to a smaller house, but it was in a better neighborhood, so I guess I shouldn't complain.

"Yeah, aight," my sister mumbled as we pulled up at our old one-story brick house, parked and walked up to the back door.

When we got inside, Big Bob was up in there drunk as hell. I knew right then that we could take his ass for everything he had and be gone in no time.

"Hey there, who are these beautiful girls?" he asked the second we walked into the house.

Ugh, I was immediately disgusted. I couldn't stand a drunk ass man. The smell was unbearable, unless you also had been drinking.

"These are my daughters Khouri and Honestii," our mother proudly introduced.

"Mmm, Khouri huh?" Big Bob slurred easing closer to me.

"Oh, hell naw ma'," I snapped stepping back further away from him.

"Watch your damn mouth KK," she scolded. I just rolled my eyes at her ass. I hated that damn nickname.

"Hello, nice to meet you." I forced the words out with a tight smile.

Honestii was still standing close to the front door. She was acting more scared than me to come near his ass.

"How are you gorgeous?" He said to her.

I could see my sister swallowing hard before she spoke. "Hey," she dryly replied.

"Look, enough with the introductions. You wanna drink KK?"

"You already know I want a drink mom."

"Can I get one too please?" Honestii chimed in.

"Um, ya ass know you don't drink," my mother teased. "But I guess I can give you a little something, but not too much."

I could tell my sister was getting annoyed with our mother because she kept biting down on her bottom lip and her nose was flared out. That was the only way you could tell that she was pissed because otherwise she hid that shit. Me on the other hand, you could always see the anger written all over my face. I could never hide it.

"Here, take this and relax," our mother urged as we all sat down and got comfortable. Well, as much as we could, considering the circumstances because dude was a fucking creep.

After about a half hour of taking shots and smoking blunts, Big Bob's ass was still up and nowhere near the verge of sleep. Drunk as hell, but still wide awake...

By that time, I was annoyed and ready to knock that muthafucka in the head with something. I didn't have time to play the waiting game.

Feeling frustrated, I gave my sister and our mother the eye to let them know that I was about to run his fucking pockets. I wasn't about to wait another second.

Easing up out of my spot in the chair, I went over on the couch and sat beside that nigga. Mom peeped shit and threw on some old school Kool & the Gang to drown out any noise.

"You feel like dancing?" I flirted with Big Bob. Of course, his perverted ass jumped right at the chance. He scooped me up in his arms and pulled me close.

"Ugh," I huffed as I wiggled to break free. That shit only caused Big Bob to tighten up his grip and draw me right back to him. That man made my skin crawl.

Soon as my body touched his, he began grinding up on me. The way he was moaning let me know his mind was somewhere else. That was when I went in for the take. Surprisingly, it was easier than I thought.

When the song was over, I flopped back on the couch and acted like everything was normal. Big Bob however, headed to the bathroom.

Waiting until he was out of sight, we began counting and dividing up the cash. That nigga had three rolls; one in his back pocket of his baggy jeans and one in each of his front ones. The total equaled more than fifteen thousand dollars. *'Now, how dumb was that to be walking around with that kind of bread in your pocket,'* I thought.

"Bitch I didn't even see you take that fuckin' money. How did you do it?" Honestii quizzed with a raised brow.

"What can I say? I got skills baby!" I boasted proudly.

After the three-way split, my sister and I were ready to bounce. Thing was, we couldn't even make it to the door good before that crazy muthafucka started flipping the fuck out.

"Which one of you bitches tried to stick me for my shit?" Big Bob shouted as he came storming out of the bathroom with his nine in hand.

"Calm down baby, ain't nobody take shit from you. You're buggin' for nothing," mom spoke attempting to plead with him.

"You a muthafuckin' lie and neither one of these little bitches is leaving up out of this house until I get my money!" He barked.

"Look you need to put that fuckin' gun down because we don't need to steal shit from your broke ass!" I cursed pushing my sister behind me. There was no way in hell I would let something happen to her.

"You a fuckin' lie! I had at least fifteen stacks on me after making a pickup, now I ain't got a damn dollar. Either y'all run me my money or we can play Russian roulette with each of you bitches lives!"

"No fuck that!" My sister shouted with tears streaming heavily down her face as she began to throw her share of the money on the floor. "You can have this shit! Just get the fuck out!"

When Big Bob turned around to Honestii with the gun aimed at her, I took the chance and snatched up my mother's aluminum bat that she had sitting beside the door. I immediately whacked his ass as hard as I could before he could shoot my sister. That drunk fucker dropped and rolled with the first blow but not before he pulled the trigger again. It totally missed my sister, but it managed to hit our mother in the side of her stomach instead.

"Nooooooo!"

Honestii and I both screamed to the top of our lungs and began to panic. My body went limp when our mothers' body dropped to the floor. Instead of rushing to her, I commenced to beating the shit out of Big Bob with the bat until he was no longer moving.

"Call somebody please!" I yelled to Honestii as she was checking for Big Bob's pulse.

"Oh, my fuckin' goodness, he's dead," she cried. "Khouri! You just killed this fuckin' man!

"Fuck that nigga! He shot ma'!" I yelled out with tears streaming down my face. My face was numb as hell. This isn't what was supposed to happen.

We both wanted to check our mother to make sure she was alright, but we were too afraid. We just stood there crying not knowing what to do next.

After several seconds passed, Honestii dialed 911 and I rushed over to my mother's side. She was unconscious and barely breathing. I held on to her hand and cried while waiting for the Police and Paramedics to arrive.

Although neither of us could stop shaking, it didn't prevent me from getting up and collecting all the money up off the floor. Hell, that was evidence that could be used against us.

As for Big Bob, I knew that we could get off on killing him because he shot our mother. That was self-defense all day, but it wasn't important. The only thing that mattered at that point was mom recovering from the gunshot wound...

"Here they come now," Khouri sang out and sniffled as we listened to the sirens grow louder.

We both got up, went to the door and opened it up as we watched the ambulance arrive. Once the paramedics rushed in and they began working on our mother immediately. After several seconds they were able to stabilize her. They then rushed her to the hospital with us tailing behind them. We prayed harder than we ever had for the whole ride...

Honestii

Drawing my cell out of my jacket pocket, I dialed Marlon and had to him call Nahmir. My sister wasn't in any shape to communicate with anyone, so I did all the talking.

"What the fuck happened?" Marlon shouted the second he rushed into the emergency waiting room and pulled me into his chest. "How is your mother and are you guys okay?"

I think Marlon's body was shaking just as bad as mine. I could tell he was nervous when he released me and checked me for wounds.

Praying that Marlon didn't question me, I held on to him tightly. The last thing he needed to know was that everything that happened had to do with us trying to rob somebody. He was totally against it and if he found out he would surely fly off about it.

"Baby, are you okay?" Marlon repeated.

"I'm okay baby," I assured looking at my sister as she rocked herself in the chair over in the corner. She had her knees up to her chest and she was staring off in a daze.

"Slim should be here..."

"I'm right here!" He shouted as he went directly to Khouri. "Baby, what happened?"

"Mom just went into surgery and the doctor said it would be a while." I informed them as we all huddled together for a little privacy.

Very quietly, I began to give them the watered-down version. Nahmir cut me off before I could finish.

"Why the fuck you ain't tell me shit Khouri?"

"It ain't like we in the same space as we used to be. I used to trust you! You used to be there for me!" She spat.

"Calm down Sis," I whispered while putting my arm around her shoulder.

Pulling her closer to me, I told her that it wasn't the time to let Nahmir have it. Hesitantly she agreed and her facial expressions softened when she looked up to face him. That nigga was damn near in tears.

"I'm here now and that's what matters." Nahmir blurted out. "You know how I feel about losing people that I care about."

He wasted no time going right back to comfort my sister. I was thankful that he was there, for the moment at least...

"Let's just sit tight and see what the doctor has to say."

"I just pray it's good news Sis," Khouri replied with a half-smile.

Everything got quiet and I began to try to change the subject, but I couldn't come up with a thing to talk about. Before I could, Marlon pulled me to a seat positioned right next to him while giving me the evil eye. I knew at the very second what was coming next.

"Please don't tell me that you and your sister were hittin' a..."

"Marlon, it wasn't like that," I lied in a whisper.

"Look, what's important right now is your mother pulling through. After she's good... then we'll talk about it. Believe me Honestii, this is a conversation well overdue. I thought after we discussed it briefly before you were done, but obviously I was wrong..."

"I thought you said we were gonna talk about it later?" I pouted with tears streaming down my face. "I hear you Marlon, but I'm just worried about my mom now." I felt terrible because that's why I didn't want to do it anyway because I had a bad vibe.

"I'm sorry baby," Marlon apologized as he wrapped his arm around me and gestured me to lay my head on his shoulder. He kissed my forehead and said not another word.

We all sat there restlessly in our own thoughts and prayers for the next six long hours. The only one that kept getting up was Khouri. She wanted some information and still no one had any for us.

"I'm going to go get a soda. Anyone want anything?" Slim asked as he stood up and stretched.

We all put in our orders and Slim went to get us all drinks. When he came back, Khouri rose to her feet and began to have a breakdown. Her screeches immediately sent chills up my spine.

"What the fuck is going on? Someone had better tell me something right the fuck now! I have been up to this fuckin' nurse's station more times than I can count! Now I want some answers!"

No sooner than she finished her last demand, the doctor stepped into the waiting area. The first thing I tried to do was read his facial expressions, but I couldn't. I didn't need to once he began his speech with an apology. We all knew right then what was up...

Life left my body, and I thought I would lose it right then and there. Khouri fainted, and it took forever to get her up. Not even the smelling salts were working.

＊＊＊＊

The next few weeks were surreal for me and my sister. It was like I was functioning, but I was numb. The only thing that kept me going was Marlon. Thank God that he had been there for me through my mother's death and funeral. He and Nahmir took care of everything. Khouri and I didn't have to lift a finger. It was a good thing too because my sister had been a total wreck. She was so distraught that she had barely come out of her room. It was tearing me up inside.

After a month of that shit I couldn't take it. I had to do something to shake Khouri up out of it. I needed her. I needed my sister...

"It's been a month, Sis. You gotta stop beating yourself up about what happened. Yes, she was our mother and we both loved her deeply, but she wouldn't want this for us. She wouldn't want you blaming yourself."

"You don't?"

"I don't blame you and I definitely don't blame myself. Mom knew what the consequences could be just like we did. If anything, I think it was a wakeup call for us to get out of the game." I expressed while I plopped myself onto her bed. "We have our whole lives ahead of us and mom would want us to do something positive. We have all the money mom had stashed plus her life insurance policy. That was more than enough to start our own business or something. You know, something legal Sis."

"Aight Sis," Khouri mumbled as she roamed around her room gathering clothing items until she had a complete outfit including accessories.

"Okay, well I'm about to go get something to eat. You want to come?" I offered as I stood to leave her room.

"No, I'm good."

"Just think about what I said KK. Can you at least do that for me?" I whined trying to get her to look at me.

"Yeah," she shrugged before turning her back to me before she disappeared into her personal bathroom. "And, can we please retire that nickname now! I've always hated that name, but now it just doesn't seem right hearing it."

"I'm sorry babe, and yes I will try my best to leave it out of my vocabulary from now on."

I left her room shaking my damn head. Khouri wasn't trying to hear shit I was saying. I knew she was just saying what I wanted to hear.

By the time I came home, that heifer had gotten up and gone out to some new spot with Nahmir's ass. The only way I found out was because my nosey ass was up on her social media. I saw all the pictures she was posting. I didn't comment like I wanted to. Instead, I waited until she came home to bust her ass.

"You just ain't gonna learn!" I fussed later that evening when she finally came home.

"Fuck you mean?" She snapped as she threw her hefty bankroll on the coffee table. "Count that shit! Yeah, I just hit this nigga for ten fuckin' racks and I'm still here! What? What the fuck I gotta be scared for?"

I rolled my eyes and shook my head. I couldn't believe my sister. She was being reckless and not even caring about the shit. She was walking in danger for sure.

'I hope this is just something she's going through. I thought to myself. *Maybe she's just doing this to cope.'*

The only thing I could think to do was to call and holler at Nahmir. I prayed that he would be on the same page as me about my sister getting out the business.

Soon as he answered he started fussing. I knew that shit was coming.

"I can't tell your sister shit! You should know that! She is gonna get money with or without me. Don't you rather me be with her so I can make sure she's safe?"

"No muthafucka! I don't want her doing the shit period! Do you understand? I need my sister! She is all that I have, and I promise you that if something ever happens to her I will personally take 'ya ass out!"

"Is that a fucking threat Honestii?"

"No bastard! That's a fuckin' promise!"

I hung up on that nigga without another word and tried to calm my ass down. I was three seconds from hopping into my car going to find his punk ass. I really didn't have the patience to deal with him. Now I could see exactly why our mother didn't like Khouri with him.

"What the hell?" I jumped as I felt the vibration in my hand only to look down and notice that it was my cell ringing.

"Hey bae," I sang into the phone.

"Hey baby, I wanted to swing by and see you. Is that cool?" Marlon requested as if something was on his mind.

"Please do," I whispered. "I'm already fresh and clean and I need a stress reliever. What you got for me baby?"

"Oh, you know exactly what I got for you. I'll be at your door in five."

After disconnecting the call, I went to check on Khouri only to find her fast asleep on top of the profits of her latest lick. My eyes were glued for a few seconds. It was just long enough to start drawing me back in. The fast money was most definitely addicting. I just had to keep reminding myself that the risk wasn't worth the reward. Hell, losing our mother was proof of that.

All I knew was that I was going to stay strong for as long as I possibly could. I needed to not only because I wanted a relationship with Marlon, but because I wanted to stay alive as well...

Khouri

After losing my mother to that fuck shit my mind had been gone for a minute. I knew that I needed to shake back so I focused solely on getting my money. My mind was right which made my grind tight.

Only thing was, Honestii was constantly in my head about calming down and doing the right thing, while Slim was right beside me egging me on. I couldn't function like that. Plus, I liked doing what I did. I didn't have to deal with people unless I was the one calling the shots.

"Sis, you really need to get that shit together before something bad happens," Honestii barked as I got dressed to go out.

"Look, I'm grown as fuck and I don't need you as my *'little sister'* telling me what the fuck is going on my way. All I need from you is your support and keep your mouth shut," I honestly told her.

"I love you sis, and I don't want to lose you to this fuckin' game like we did mommy," Honestii said crying like she did when she was a little girl. It immediately got to me.

"I'm so sorry baby. Maybe I'll slow down, but for now I gotta get this money. What I didn't tell you was that mom had so much debt that the government took all the money we had in our joint account. Those grimey ass muthafuckas took everything but seven hundred dollars plus took both of the houses!"

"I know you betta be lying!" Honestii snapped becoming even more emotional.

"I wish I was sis. Why you think I've been busting my ass to make these moves?" I asked her. "I do this shit to make sure we're alright boo! You're my lil' sister and I love you, but this is all we have right now."

"And I love you more big head," she told me while coming to give me a hug.

When she let me loose, I hit her with the sad eyes. I had to show her how serious I was.

"Are you coming with me tonight? I need you," I pleaded.

I knew that if I told her that I needed her she would more than likely come with me. I had to go. Shit, that was the only thing that kept my mind off the so called *'one-time cheating'* and my mother's death. They both were driving me crazy.

"KK, I really would rather us to stay in tonight and watch movies or something. It has been way too long since we actually spent some time together without going out here scamming niggas."

I thought about what she was saying, but my mind was way too focused on the money. I had to keep it that way so I wouldn't break down in tears.

"I get what you're saying baby, and I don't mind sitting in and taking a day off, but let's just go out tonight and I promise that I will calm it down for a few weeks after this."

"If I agree to go with you then we're not going to the club. As bad as I hate to say it, we can go over ya nigga house where I know we'll at least be safe. I can't stand his ass right about now, but I will go over there with you just this once Sis." Honestii smiled at me and I knew that I had her right where I wanted her.

Silently, I hoped that if she was in that environment then she would hit one good jug with me. Then, I thought maybe she would at least be open and want to get back in the swing of things. I didn't want to the shit solo. We were a team.

Sure, I had Nahmir, but it wasn't the same. With my sister it was certain of the bond. With Nahmir, I wasn't so sure. I was most definitely in love with him, but I found myself still struggling with my feelings.

I couldn't talk to my sister about it because all she wanted was to judge me. She was still mad as hell at him for stepping out with Bella's ass. I understood her feelings, but she didn't understand mine. I was becoming obsessively in love with Nahmir and even though I was able to suppress it on the outside, I had no control of how it took over on the inside.

"I really don't want Marlon to know," my sister whined causing my thoughts of Nahmir to temporarily fade away.

"Damn, is he your keeper?" I huffed. "That is just your boyfriend, not your fuckin' daddy!"

"No, but he is my man, that boyfriend shit is childish!" She snapped with no hesitation. She was defending Marlon's ass to the 'T' and it caught me off guard. I had always been number one in my little sister's life so for her to go against me to please her so called 'man'.

I wasn't salty about her falling for Marlon in no way shape or form. What I had a problem with was the way he always tried to persuade my sister to stop doing what we did best. He was really starting to get on my damn nerves with that bullshit. Honestii needed to stop listening to his ass and realize that she had a mind of her own.

We both had that shit bad. She couldn't stand Nahmir and I couldn't stand Marlon's ass half of the time. They both constantly stayed in our damn business like they didn't have any of their own.

It seemed like things only got worse after losing our mother. Ever since then we were always in a battle with one another over petty shit. Shit, my sister was right. We most needed some peace.

Shaking my thoughts, I continued with the conversation I was holding with my sister. I let her know that I was supposed to go over to Nahmir's after the club anyway.

"I'll just skip the club and we can go straight to Slim's."

"I heard his shit wasn't open last weekend though."

"No, he was out of town supposedly on business," I smirked with my head turned. I didn't want Honestii trying to read me.

"Well, is he having his usual get together tonight?"

"Yeah," I told her when I wasn't sure myself. "Let's just go over there and see what's jumping off."

"Okay, that's cool with me. I'll call him and see what's up." I assured my sister and I got up and dug in my purse until I found my cell.

Immediately dialing Nahmir up, I made sure everything was going on as usual. Once he verified it, I gave my sister the head nod, hung up then turned around to shove my phone back down in my MK bag.

"You really love that sorry ass nigga, huh?" Honestii asked with a frown.

Her question threw me, so it took a few seconds to respond. "Why you ask that?"

"That fuckin' smile you wore the whole time you were on the phone with him," she huffed with her arms folded across her chest as she shifted all of her weight to one side. Hell, I honestly didn't realize I was smiling.

"Whatever just go do what you have to do and be ready when it's time to leave," I reminded as I saw her ass right on up out of my room. I had shit to do myself...

****

Later that night when we made it to Nahmir's crib, it was dry as fuck. I didn't know where everybody was, but we weren't going to stay too long if it didn't pick up. In the meantime, we had a couple of drinks and chilled.

While I downed shots of Apple Jack, Honestii slowly sipped her wine. She was being extremely quiet, but I didn't bother her. I just continued to get lit until it livened up.

Finally, after about an hour or so, people started to show. The turnout was better than usual before too long. By that time, Honestii was able to enjoy herself more. I was positive that the alcohol helped.

"What's going on baby? You gotta tell me how you got ya sister to get out the crib and over to my spot. The last time I talked to her she was cursing my ass out," he spoke jokingly bending down to kiss my lips. He only did that shit because Honestii was sitting nearby and he knew it would annoy her, especially since he knew that she didn't want us together.

"Now you know I have the gift of gab baby. I just told her ass that I would take off work for a little while if she came out with me, but her ass didn't wanna hit the club. Believe it or not, she was the one who suggested that we come over here."

Nahmir's eyes narrowed as he glared at me. "What?" I questioned him about the way he was eyeing me down as if he was accusing me of something.

"What the fuck are y'all up to?" He quizzed as he drew back from the hold, he had me hemmed up in.

"Excuse me boss, where should I put these?" A young half naked chick asked while tapping him on the shoulder.

Both Honestii and I looked at each other and then to the girl. "Who the hell is *that bitch*?" my sister mouthed as she stepped to my table. It sent the chick scurrying off. I couldn't help but to burst out in laughter. That shit was funny as hell.

"I just hired her. She's a lil' cutie, huh?" Slim teased as he stepped to me and kissed my lips then whispered in my ear. "How about we have a lil' party after this shit dies down in here?"

"What's in it for me besides some dick?" I questioned in a hushed tone.

"I might have a surprise for you," he whispered sticking his tongue in my ear.

My heart raced in anticipation as Nahmir patted his pants pocket. He then smiled and gave me that hungry look.

"You want me?"

"Yeah baby, you know it's been a minute. Why you keep holding out?" he whispered.

"Because..."

'I guess not getting none of this good-good is starting to get to that ass.'

"Because what?"

"Don't worry about that right now. Just tell me who's working my table tonight?" I inquired hoping that he would say nobody. Since I had my little sis with me, I figured I would work the Blackjack table on the low. I didn't want her to know I was about to be on my bullshit.

"Now you know don't nobody get on my shit but you and my Auntie, but since you're here with me she can work the Tunk table, so that you can get down tonight. You already know we're about to kill 'em too," he said grabbing me into a tight hug, then walking off.

That nigga was really starting to act like he cared about me. I knew the little bit of time passing with him not getting this good wet pussy would eventually straighten his ass up. I just didn't know for how long.

"Damn Sis it's lit up in this bitch," Honestii shouted walking up behind me. "You about to work the tables?"

"Yeah," I said heading to relieve Nahmir's aunt. My sister was right on my heels. I knew she wanted to make sure that I wasn't hitting nobody's pockets. I wasn't. Instead I was about to hit them another way. My sister just wasn't up on game.

"Okay, I'm gonna just stand here and watch," Honestii informed me as she eyed the cards that I was dealing.

It didn't take long for her to start complaining that her feet were hurting. I tried to tell her ass not to wear those damn heels, but this heffa couldn't go nowhere without them.

"Go sit down Sis," I suggested and motioned my head towards the sofas positioned against the far-right wall.

At first it seemed like Honestii was going to fight her pain but after a few more minutes she was tapping out and took them damn shoes off. I didn't give a damn long as she went away so I could get my hustle on.

She was blocking for a while, but after she left me at the table, I began working my magic. Turning my head in a full circle, I scanned the room searching for my next victim. It didn't take long for the next sucker to walk up.

I just stayed quiet and smiled as he drew his wad of cash out of his pocket. I could tell he was drunk already so I let him do all the talking.

"I'm about to tear this table up!" the ugly nigga shouted as he laid his money down aggressively and began talking shit. I just ignored him and began hitting his ass hard.

Now, while I was taking this fool for his bread on the table, Ruga, a nigga I knew in high school walked up trying to spit some game on me. It had been since my freshmen year that I had last seen him. He was a senior then.

I hardly recognized him that night. His appearance had changed for the better.

"Hey Khouri, what you been up to?"

"Nothing just on these tables. What about you? How have you been?" I asked as I peeped his gear. I couldn't front, dude had really come up since we were in school.

"Shit baby, just out here getting this fucking money. You know I started off hustling rides I stole, but I got my own car lot now, legit and everything. I had to make that big paper so that I could take care of my queen when I found her.

"Oh yeah?"

"Yeah queen, now maybe you'll give a real king a shot at loving you."

"Ruga, you still be trippin'," I blushed a bit playing coy but only with thoughts of running his pockets. "It's good to hear that you're doing well though."

"Yo, I heard about your mother man. That shit was fucked up."

"Thanks, so much Ruga. I really appreciate that. I miss her so much man. Shit hasn't been the same since she been gone."

"Yeah, I can't even imagine."

Damn, Ruga really had me going when he flashed his cash and bragged on what he had. Yeah, the nigga was fine and all, but the green looked way better than he did. Besides, my heart was already with Nahmir and nobody could change that.

I was so busy plotting how to get Ruga that I almost start slipping on the table. I couldn't take that loss.

"Hold on just a second," I requested as I looked around trying to find Nahmir's aunt so that she could come and relieve me.

I needed her to come run the table so that I could reel Ruga all the way in. I wanted to be able to focus so that I could get close enough to him to see what kind of capital he was really working with.

"Let's go over here so that we can have some more privacy?" I suggested while leading him to my favorite dark corner.

"Oh, I'm right behind ya ass," he whispered close enough for me to smell the alcohol and mint on his breath.

I'm not gonna lie, that shit was getting my pussy a little wet.

I stayed on Ruga's ass hard and before we left, I had run his pockets for a stack. On top of that shit, I had a date with him the next night.

Once he was out of sight, I went to count my money because I was ready to bounce. "Damn, six thousand?"

I couldn't believe that shit. It was a great night, but I was ready for it to end. I was tired and all I wanted to do was to wrap up with my man and give him what he had been missing.

Hurrying to find Nahmir, I peeled him off a couple of thousand I made off the table then confirmed our plans for later. Then I went off to find my sister. I just knew she was ready to go...

"I'm ready KK," she smiled and put her jacket on. "I actually had a good time and I see you did too," she spoke pointing to Ruga's ass

I couldn't escape that damn nickname for the life of me. I wanted to spaz, but I let it slide. "Yeah, that was Ruga. Remember him from school?"

"No, he must have graduated before I started high school KK." She joked. "He looks like he has some cash though. So, what's up? Are you gonna fuck 'wit 'em?"

"Me?"

"Yeah you...," she taunted as she side-eyed me. "Unless you already have a man."

"Whatever," I sighed as I grabbed her arm. "Let's go."

I honestly just wanted to drop her off and get right back to Nahmir's ass. I saw how that new bitch he hired was on him and I wasn't about to let that shit go down. I had been through way too much to lose him. He was mine...

Honestii

"Damn, I'm tired!" I sighed as I climbed into my bed and debated about hitting Marlon up.

He had been blowing up my cell since I was at Nahmir's spot. I knew that he probably had an attitude and I really didn't have the patience to be dealing with him right then.

Shit, I was tipsy and ready to count my money. Yes, I knew that I said I wasn't going to do any more scamming, but I couldn't help myself once we got there and I got to drinking. Shit, after I got a good buzz going, stealing was like second nature.

Once I hit this bitches' purse for that little change, I was on a roll. I couldn't wait to see what my total was.

I was real sneaky about it though because I didn't want my sister to catch me. Instead I kept it to myself right along with all the cash I had lifted.

"Three, four, five thousand three hundred dollars," I chanted softly. I was just that much closer to buying my own house. My sister and I were tight as fuck and thick as thieves, but with her nigga acting like he didn't want her on the same shit I was on, made me want my own spot. I needed to move on my own.

Now that was what I called a night. I should have been ashamed of myself, especially once I began sobering up.

Sitting down in the chair, I threw my head in my hands and cried. I had to stop and so did my sister.

'Knock, Knock'

Khouri pounded on my door two good times before busting in. I didn't even have enough time to hide my ends.

"Oh, hell nah! Don't tell me you made all that tonight? You a little sneaky muthafucka!" My sister said jokingly.

Feeling bad for hiding it from her, I offered her half. When she turned it down, I knew it was because she had to have made a hefty come up her damn self. She wasn't fooling nobody, especially me. Tuh, Khouri never turned money down for no reason.

"I'm cool," she smiled before leaving my room. "I just wanted to come and tell you that I love you Sis."

"I love you more...," I tried to reply before she slammed my door shut.

She blew me a kiss and left. I adored the relationship we had, and I thanked God every night for her, especially now that we had lost our mother.

'Let me get out of my feelings and call my man,' I thought.

Grabbing my cell, I dialed Marlon. Soon as he answered he let me have it. I knew I had it coming so I just listened attentively.

"Okay, now that you're done fussing at me, can you come by and see me, daddy?" he loved when I called him that, so I figured he would be open.

"You know I can, hell, I've been by your house about a dozen times! I didn't even think to look for your ass at Nahmir's spot! *Since you did say you were done 'wit that!*"

"Are you coming over or not?"

"I'm on my way, man!" He assured before harassing me a bit more. "You love me?"

"Huh?" I giggled trying to play it off so I wouldn't have to answer.

"You heard me," Marlon repeated. "Do you love me?"

"I'm not sure…" I stuttered a little bit…as I giggled.

"Aight then," he sighed. "If you don't…"

"What? What are you trying to say?" I played dumb.

"I'm trying to tell you Honestii…"

"What?"

"You know what… I'm gonna make you love me girl!" He barked disconnecting the call.

Marlon's words shot through me like a lightning bolt. It was so powerful that it had me wanting him even more.

"Ah, you are?"

"Yes, now I'm on my way baby," he spoke seductively before hanging up. He made sure not to give me a chance to object.

So, okay, Marlon lived only a few short miles away from us so my time for freshening up was limited. I was able to make the most of it and I was answering the door not even twenty minutes later.

"Why are you wearing that freaky shit baby?" Marlon quizzed as he got right up on me and began sniffing me.

"You like it daddy?" I giggled as the tip of his nose tickled my neck. "Aht, Aht bae."

When Marlon drew back, he snatched my wrist and pulled me onto the bed with him making me gasp for a second. I quickly shook it off and nestled into his arms. Everything was so quiet, peaceful, and it made my pussy jump with every touch he delivered to my supple body.

Several seconds later, the silence was broken by Marlon bringing up old memories. He began about the first night I met him, and I lied about my age. He found out the next week when he came up to my school looking for me.

"I should've left ya young ass alone then," he teased. "But, something about you hooked my ass!"

"Then we wouldn't be together now," I told his ass.

"I waited over a year for you without touching another girl! Do you know any man that would do some shit like that?" he whispered with a grin while staring me in my eyes. I swear anytime someone did that it made me nervous.

"Naw, who?" I replied nervously as I tried miserably to keep a straight face.

"Oh, now you got jokes, huh? You remember the night of your birthday when I got to tear that ass up?"

"Maybe, I don't know," I stalled while watching him stand to his feet.

"Well, why don't I refresh your memory?" Marlon requested as he began removing his clothes.

"Please do," I seductively replied.

I lay there while admiring his body as each item dropped to the floor simultaneously. Every inch of this man was so defined to perfection. I swear he was made just for me. Just the sight of him had me salivating. I was ready for everything and anything that he was about to give me...

Marlon was fine from his arms to his chest, to his abs down to his thick nine inches that hung down below. That shit right there was the business and he damn sure knew how to use it.

"Come here and give it to me baby!" I purred with my eyes. He read them and began easing slowly towards my inner thick thighs.

Taking his time to climb on top of me, he hovered over me before kissing me. He then lifted my nightie and dove right into my *'panty less-pussy'* face first.

Just as we were getting into it, I gestured for him to roll me on top. As he positioned me to ride his face backwards, I gripped his thighs for more leverage as I swayed my hips backwards then forward...constantly. As my pussy dripped with my creamy juices, he moaned gripping my ass. I moved aggressively against his face until he gulped my sweet nectar...repeatedly.

"Oh, ah, shit..." his groans were muffled as he shoved his tongue even deeper inside of my juicy morsel. The combination was just enough to put me in the mood to taste my man.

"Ooooo wait baby," I whispered and adjusted my body the opposite way and leaned down until my lips touched the head of his thick dick.

"Mmmmm," he hummed as he regained his grip on my clit.

I got straight to business and wrapped my mouth around the head. I then twirled my tongue around it as I jerked my neck back and forth. Soon as his moans became increasingly louder, I pulled it out my mouth, looked him in his eyes and spit on it.

"Oh my God, baby! I fuckin' love you!" he panted.

"Mmmm," I moaned and broke him down with a double combo twist three thousand baby. I have never seen him act like that before. That man was squirming all over the bed.

After about a minute or two, I could tell that he was about to bust. The veins pulsating in his dick set that alarm off for me. I tightened my grip and sucked harder and faster until he shot his babies down my throat.

Without a heads up, I released his monster from my mouth slowly.

"Damn, why you do that baby?" He whined. "You just sucked the soul out of my shit."

Instead of replying, I kissed the head of his dick and straddled him.

Marlon sat up a bit and watched what was going on below. "You like this shit, don't you?" I teased seductively.

"Cum for me baby, come for daddy!" he begged as he took his fingers and fondled my clit while he continued to penetrate me at a slow pace.

With his other hand, he massaged my breasts and increased his thrust upward to meet my every grind. The feeling was incredible and had my body shaking like crazy as I had back to back orgasms.

Before I could calm myself down, Marlon was back at it but more aggressively. This time I was going all in and began helping him fondle me. I was placing his hands in all the places I wanted him to touch until he hit my spot. "Oh, right there, daddy," I pleaded.

"Right there?"

"Yes daddy! Yes, right there."

"Damn, I love you. I love you baby," He repeated those same words over and over until I opened my eyes and locked them with his. "I love you Honestii."

I didn't answer him. My body was still shaking. I had to get my thoughts together...

Khouri

When it came time for my date with Ruga the next day, my heart was jumping like crazy and I didn't know why. It wasn't like it was a blind date, or I was going out with a stranger. I knew this guy and his history. I think my nervousness was coming from the fact that he didn't know me and my background.

"Hey Sis, Ruga is on his way to come get me. I'll see you when I get back!" I yelled from my room.

"Unt uh, you said that you were gonna chill after last night KK," Honestii said busting up in my bedroom.

"Oh, here ya ass go! I'm not doing shit girl, it's just a date, so relax," I hissed.

"I know ya ass and ain't shit just a date with you. Not to mention that you just snatched some stacks off his ass last night."

"Honestii please shut that shit up and worry about ya nigga, and the way he had that ass moaning last night. Yeah, I heard all ten minutes of that shit," I told her jokingly.

I knew that if me going out with Ruga wouldn't shut her ass up, then mentioning that her ass sounded like a wounded animal the night before would. My little sister hated talking about her sex life.

"You know what, fuck it Khouri. Do what you do. I swear ya ass is so damn hardheaded that it doesn't even make sense," Honestii spat walking back to her room.

I wasn't about to chase her down and try to baby her ass that time. She was starting to get on my damn nerves with all of that *'calm down'* shit anyway.

Ignoring her ass totally, I picked up my cell and dialed Ruga to make sure he was on his way.

"What's up beautiful?" He answered.

"Hey, are you on the way yet?"

"I'm about to pull up now. Damn girl, what you got, GPS on a nigga?" He joked.

"Whatever bye, I'm on the way out," I said disconnecting the call.

At first, I didn't want to tell him where I lived. I didn't need him coming back and trying no crazy shit. Then I figured what the hell. I wasn't scared of his little ass.

****

When Ruga pulled up to Ruth Chris Restaurant out in the suburbs, my ass got low key excited because I had never been to such a fancy place. Now don't get it fucked up, I could splurge on myself daily at spots like that one, but I'd rather cook my own meal.

"You like their food?" Ruga asked with a smug look on his face like he knew that I had never eaten there before.

"No, I haven't tried it before," I admitted as we sat in his ride and chatted for a bit.

"Good, I'm sure you'll like it," Ruga flirted then turned it into a frown before he spoke again. "Oh, I didn't tell you, but last night at Slim spot I lost like two stacks. That's the last time I'm going back over that bitch."

I knew right away that he was cappin' hard as fuck. I had only got his ass for a band, and nothing more. Shit, I knew Honestii didn't get him, so that shit was dead. I ain't gonna lie though, my heart sank to my coochie when he said that because I was the guilty party. I couldn't even swallow. I knew I had to think quick on my feet.

"Damn nigga, I guess gambling isn't your thing, huh?"

"Hell nah, I lost that shit just walking around that bitch, or I got robbed. I ain't worried 'bout that shit doe," he announced. "Plus, I got much more where that came from.

"Oh, for real."

"Come on let's get up in here and eat up this food," he told me as he got out the car.

When we got inside of the restaurant, Ruga was all over me. I didn't know what was on his mind, but he damn sure wasn't getting no pussy. This shit belonged to Nahmir and only him.

I already had it in my mind, if he tried to smash, I would use that ninety-day rule shit...quick. Knowing good and damn well that our little fling wasn't going to last nearly that long.

The only reason that I even agreed to see his ass after lickin' him was because I was curious about the kind of money he was holding for real. Other than that, it was an ordinary date; no intimate feelings whatsoever.

I swear all I could think about the whole time was Nahmir's ass. I was wearing myself out not giving him any. I needed that shit bad as fuck.

"Here is some lemon water," the waiter said as he placed two tall glasses onto the table. "I'll be right back to take your order."

When it came time to pick what I wanted to eat off that expensive ass menu, I was stuck like chuck. I didn't wanna seem like a thirsty ass chick, and order up a bunch of shit, so I had to play shit off.

"Oh my God Ruga, there is so much to choose from that I don't even know what to order," I whined.

"Girl don't even trip. This is how I eat all the time and now that you're fucking with me, this is how you'll be eating more often," he boasted.

"If you say so Ruga," I giggled. "I'm hungry and I don't want to order a lot of stuff that I'm not going to eat."

"Get anything you want Khouri. Get three entrees' if you want to baby. Today is all about you."

"Awww, thank you," I smiled on the outside but was still stuck on what to order. This nigga was starting to make me feel like a princess. I can't front because I was loving this shit. Nahmir never did shit like that.

I took another look at my menu and said fuck it. I ordered Calamari for the appetizer, then I had a Caribbean Lobster Tail for my entrée, and I had a glass of Malbec, a red wine that originated in France. The last thing that nigga should have done was to tell me to order what I wanted.

"So, are you gonna fuck wit' 'cha boy now that I got my shit together?" Ruga asked taking a sip from his glass.

"We can see where things go. I'm sure you have women lined up at your door and I don't wanna step on anyone's toes," I told him with a hint of sarcasm.

"Come on now Khouri, you know that's not how I get down. Now, don't get it fucked up. Mad bitches be at ya boy, but all they want is a couple of dollars and a free meal," he explained. "I'm trying to fuck with you on that deep spiritual and mental shit."

'Oh, hell nah, this nigga really trippin'. It ain't even that deep,' I thought.

There was not a chance in hell that I would ever get on that level with Ruga, but I would play along because that 'Lick' all together would be well worth my time. That I did know...

"I mean I'm feeling you, but I don't want to jinx it either. Let's just take things one day at a time," I said trying to slow him down a bit.

"Well, long as you're giving me that much, I'll take it," Ruga said holding his wine glass up in the air to clink with mine.

Once we got that topic out of the way, we sat there and kicked it. We spoke about old times and had some real good laughs before leaving the restaurant.

When we got in the car, Ruga put on some smooth R & B and I got cozy in my seat. That was up until he passed the exit to my crib. My senses immediately went on high alert.

"Hold up, where are we going?" I quizzed popping up in my seat.

"Chill baby, I don't want the date to end just yet. Let's go to the Aquarium."

My nerves settled and I was a little impressed. I hadn't been there before, but it was on my 'to-do-list'.

"Oh, that's cool," I agreed reclining my seat back a little bit.

We pulled up to the stop light across the street from our destination, and I looked over only to meet eyes with Nahmir's ass. At first, he grilled me, but he quickly changed it up when I smirked. His expression suddenly turned into a look of sadness, but I didn't care. I wanted him to feel like I had when he cheated on me with that ugly ass heifer. It served his ass right!

I politely turned myself back around in my seat and acted like he didn't even fucking exist. I wasn't about to let him spoil my mood. Hell, I was having a good time with Ruga and I wasn't about to be rude.

As we pulled away, I saw Nahmir pull his cell out and began dialing. I knew he was about to ring my phone so before that nigga even had the chance to call me, I powered my phone off. Not today Satan...

Honestii

While Marlon and I had been kicking it hard for the past few weeks, my sister was continuing to avoid having sex with Ruga. I knew she couldn't have liked him too much because she was still stuck on Nahmir. She didn't think I knew but I did.

"What's up Sis," I greeted as I came in the house early in the morning after being out all night with Marlon.

Khouri was in the kitchen making some breakfast. She usually didn't cook so my interest peaked right away.

"Who is all that food for?"

"Ruga stayed over last night so I thought I'd get up early and whip us up some grub," she answered nonchalantly.

I scooted a high stool up to the counter and began to stare my sister down. I knew that she felt me looking at her, but she dared to glance my way.

There were a dozen questions brewing in my head, but only one came out of my mouth. As soon as I released it Khouri snapped.

"Just because the nigga slept in my bed, don't mean I let him slip in my pussy!" She fussed.

I couldn't understand why she was tripping. She had been seeing Ruga damn near every day for almost a month. Sleeping with him shouldn't have been a big deal.

Suddenly I heard footsteps coming down the hallway. Seconds later Ruga appeared in his *'wife-beater'* and basketball shorts. The expression on his face let me know that he wasn't expecting to see me in the kitchen.

"Good Morning y'all," he greeted as he walked directly towards my sister and wrapped his arms around her from behind.

After kissing her neck, he smiled and told me that he was going to have my sister. Khouri didn't object so I wanted to further explore his intentions.

"So, are you saying that you want to be with her? Are you saying that you're in love with my sister?"

"Honestii don't start!" my sister smirked. "Just because you and Marlon are all lovey-dovey, don't drag us into it."

"She's not dragging me into shit baby," Ruga flirted as he turned Khouri towards him. "I do love you baby and no matter how much you deny returning the same feelings for me, I know. Yeah, I know that you love a nigga so stop with the games."

Ruga didn't let her say a word. He touched his finger to her lips and told her, "Hold that thought baby." Then he ran off to the other room and came right back holding a medium sized box.

"Stop buying me stuff Ruga," she huffed as I stood there watching, just wondering how things were about to unfold.

Ignoring my sister, Ruga opened the box and pulled out two smaller boxes. "Here, open this first."

Slowly obeying his command, my sister took the lid off the red box and drew out a keychain with three keys on it. "What are these?"

Reaching out to explain, Ruga showed my sister key, by key and told her what they were for. I was truly impressed to say the fucking least.

"One is to the property that I just bought on the east side. The paperwork in the box will prove that your name is on all the documents right along with mine. One is to our safety deposit box and the last one is to your whip that's parked in the garage at the new house."

"I don't understand," Khouri gasped as she accepted the keychain from Ruga right along with the remaining unopened box.

"Now what is this?"

I had a feeling what was coming next. My hands were sweating from anticipation like I was getting the damn gift. It was just as good though because I loved to see my sister happy.

"Is this a..." she stuttered as she held the large diamond solitaire ring in the air and stared at it with an amazed look.

Ruga removed it from her hand and placed it on her ring finger. "Yes, it is baby. I need to know if you love me and if you want to make this shit official?"

"Official like what?" She tried to have him clarify. "Not official like in marriage? We haven't even been intimate. Hell, we only been kicking it for a few weeks."

"I know and that makes me love you even more. You are like no other woman I have ever been with Khouri. I don't just want you in my life. I need you in it."

"I'm flattered beyond words, but this is going a little bit too fast Ruga. I'm scared."

"Don't be scared baby, you are everything that I've ever wanted. Just think about it, baby," Ruga begged.

By the look in his eyes, I knew he was being sincere. I truly felt sorry for him because he had no idea what he was up against. My sister was too stuck on Nahmir's raggedy ass.

Tears began to stream down my sister's face and that was a rarity for her. That was my cue to leave the kitchen. I took my ass right to my room and dialed Marlon. I had to tell him what just happened. Hopefully that would make him step his game up too because he hadn't even mentioned a future with me. At least not long term, and we had been kicking it longer...

"So, what you sound a little salty baby," he teased. "You got a man that loves you and will do anything for you. Why are you tripping?"

"I'm not," I pouted feeling a little left out. "I just thought..."

"You just thought what?" Marlon questioned. "You can't even tell me you love me when I need to hear it."

"Never mind, it wasn't important."

He didn't press me for an explanation. He just changed the subject and asked if I wanted to go to lunch. I really wasn't hungry, so I told him to come and get me in a few hours.

I plopped down onto my bed and sighed. I was bored and ready to get into something. I hadn't had any real excitement in a while. Marlon had been on me about the shit me and my sister was into, so I had nothing to do.

An idea suddenly popped into my head. I rushed into my closet and changed my clothes. I grabbed my car keys and went and hopped in my ride.

"Where can I go at this time of morning?" I contemplated as I pulled off and headed straight to the freeway.

I had no idea where my destination was. I just wanted to get out of the house.

Since I had been hanging tough with Marlon, I had been doing more spending money than making money. I was going to the spa, salon and casino like I had an endless bank card.

Of course, Marlon had warned me time and time again that he would pay for everything everywhere we went, but that shit got old. I liked to pay my own way sometimes, plus treat my man to a good time.

I guess it was time for me to step up and get a damn job. That was the only thing that made sense.

'Beep, beep, beep'

Suddenly the warning light on my dash caught my attention, letting me know that I was low on fuel. Not wanting to push it, I got off on the next exit and went to the first gas station I saw.

"Hello gorgeous," the tall handsome foreign guy greeted as I got out of my car.

"Oh, hello," I replied shyly being taken by his strong accent.

That fine ass muthafucka was pushing a brand-new Benz that didn't even have the plates on it yet. It was all blue and clean as fuck. The chrome was so shiny that it was reflecting every light that was illuminated.

"Are you from around here?" He asked politely. "I'm looking for a good place to get some food."

"Yes, I live not too far from here. What do you have a taste for?"

I flirted with only one thing on my mind; money. But, why did he have to stare at me and lick his fucking lips? I swear he was so sexy. From his clean-shaven face, to his casual attire, all the way to his foreign swag he was an eye catcher.

"Some pancakes and sausage," he replied with a smile showing his gold trimmed tooth on the side. "Would you like to join me?"

You know a bitch like me jumped all over that shit; especially when everything about him screamed *'cash'*. I parked my ride and hopped in the car with him. I made sure I had my mini stun gun just in case because I was taking a risk that I normally wouldn't have taken. *'What was I thinking?'*

Now, while in the car, I played the shy role all the way to the restaurant and through the meal. It wasn't until we got a little tipsy that he got bold and started feeling me up.

That shit was so disrespectful that I had to get his ass. I knew it was wrong, but he was asking for it. Shit, I wasn't a prostitute, and he wasn't about to treat me like one. Period!

Man, I was in and out of his pockets so fast that he didn't know what was going on. Soon as I accomplished my mission, I excused myself from the table and told him that I was going to the bathroom. I used that opportunity to call a taxi. I was up out of that bitch and back to my car within the next thirty minutes.

Yeah, I still had it, but I needed help. I really had to stop because after that one, I realized that I couldn't help myself...

Khouri

I was kind of thrown for a loop at Ruga's indecent proposal. I mean shit, how was I supposed to say yes to marriage when I was still in love with that trifflin' ass Nahmir. I needed to get my head together and focus on trying to stick that nigga for his paper instead of falling for his *'sweet talk'*. Well, I guess I can't say talk since this man showed me paper, but let's be real. I wasn't even twenty years old yet.

"So why are you not trying to answer my question?" Ruga inquired with a sneering look on his face.

"It's not that I don't want to answer Ruga. That question just came out of left field. I do love you," I lied. "I'm just scared that we're moving too fast. I don't want to ever say that I got a divorce. I take marriage very seriously."

Ruga was pressing my ass and I didn't know what else to tell him. The only thing left for me to do was throw him some old made up bullshit that came to the top of my head.

"I feel what you're saying, but I know what it is with us. Besides, who ever said that we would get a divorce baby," Ruga said pulling me close and kissing my forehead.

"Well since you put it like that then I guess I can say yes," I replied with a half ass concocted smile. I didn't give two fucks what I told him. That nigga wasn't about to stop my money train. Besides that, he was being aggie as fuck, so I just agreed to shut his ass the hell up.

Ruga took my hand and gazed at the ring he had placed there. He looked so sincere that I almost felt sorry for him.

'This nigga couldn't possibly think that I would marry him!' I laughed inward.

There were no intentions on my part to make a commitment to Ruga, let alone exchange vows with him. If I did that it would interfere with me running his pockets and I couldn't have that...

****

Probably twenty minutes or so later, Honestii came waltzing in the door with a big ass grin on her face. I already knew what time it was. The only thing that could produce that type of smile was getting some dick or hitting a fucking lick.

"Come here Sis. I got something for ya," she urged.

"Look baby, I gotta roll out. Call me later," Ruga told me while slapping my ass as he walked towards the door.

"Okay bye baby," I replied as I went behind him and locked up.

After turning back around, I walked towards my sister. I was just about to bust her ass out, but before I could she had to tried to clown me.

"Oh, I see ya ass is sporting that dope ass ring now. I guess you said yes," she teased.

"I did, but on another note bitch. The next time Ruga's ass is over don't be so damn giddy about this scamming shit. You know that nigga don't have a clue as to what we're doing so watch out with all that. I can't have that shit right now."

Honestly in my heart of hearts I was feeling Ruga, but I was scared that he would turn out like Nahmir. Either way, I knew that I was going to be stuck between a rock and a hard place if I didn't get my shit together.

"Oh, girl shit, he didn't know what the fuck I was talking about. Fuck all that and look at this shit," Honestii demanded pulling out a large wad of money.

"Who the fuck did you knock off bitch?" I asked with a raised brow.

"Don't you worry your pretty little head about that. Just know that I have a few dollars for you," Honestii spoke passing me two hundred fifty dollars.

I took the money she gave me and stuck it in my bra. It didn't quite fit in there, but it would have to do until I got a chance to put that shit up.

"Come up to my room, I have something to show you."

"What you gotta show me?" Honestii inquired while steady on my heels.

"Don't worry about it, just follow me," I urged.

When we arrived at my bedroom, I switched the light on because my drapes weren't pulled. It was pitch black up in there.

"Damn Dracula," Honestii joked.

"Oh hush."

My sister took a seat on the chair beside my bed and I went over to the closet and retrieved a red bag. When I dumped the contents on the bed my sister jumped up and covered her mouth.

"Oh my God KK, what the fuck are you doing with those two big ass guns?"

"Girl hush, we are about to set shit off! We're not making enough money, and this is a sure way to get it. All we have to do is run up in a couple of houses, lick their ass and we're set for life!"

"I'm not with the gun play Sis. Besides, I thought we were quitting?" My sister reminded.

"Did you really just say that dumb shit after you just did practically the same shit?"

"That was my last one Sis, honestly."

"Whatever, you said that shit a million times Honestii..."

"It doesn't matter because what we are NOT gonna do is stick anyone up with a fuckin' gun!" She barked. "Why would you even need heat like that?"

"Because this is the best way to handle shit. Damn why can't you just go with me on this Honestii?"

"KK, you know that I'm always down for you, but this is crazy! It's just how we lost mommy," she cried.

I walked over to the chair my sister was sitting and tightly wrapped my arms around her. "Honestii, don't cry baby. I know that is how we lost mommy, but I promise that we won't hurt anybody. The guns are only for insurance purposes. You know, so that we don't get hurt ourselves. I'm tired of picking pockets. It's time to get down."

My sister sniffled a little bit and wiped the tears from her face before she spoke.

"I understand what you're saying, but this scares me, it would kill me if something happened to you. Shit, my mental would be all fucked up."

"Before we do anything, I'll make sure we have all of our bases covered."

"No, I'm totally against it, KK!"

"Well, I'm gonna do this shit with or without you!" I told her trying to force her hand.

"No, you're not!"

"You can't fuckin' stop me Khouri so you might as well just come and have my back!"

"Oh, so you are just gonna go by yourself?" Honestii snapped. "Are you gonna at least take Nahmir?"

"Slim don't know shit about this! I don't wanna split my shit with him! You're my sister! We need this!"

"No, we don't!"

"Yes, the fuck we do, and I promise you Sis, I'm doing this either way it goes. Even if it means doing it solo!"

After going over it in her head, Honestii was ready to compromise.

"I will only go along with this if you promise me that we will only use the guns if it is absolutely necessary," she warned. "And this has to be it Sis! I don't wanna lose you or Marlon because if he finds out he's gonna leave me this time. I meant it KK! This has to be the last one!"

"I promise to the high heavens Sis."

That being said. We hugged it out and headed back downstairs for drinks. Even though it was early I was ready to get lit and relax.

While were talking, I let my little sister know that I had planned for us to spend that evening at Nahmir's hot spot. We needed to relax and lay low.

"You better take that big ass rock off ya finger before Slim flip all the way out."

"Girl, I'm not worried about his ass, but I am gonna put it away for the time being. Shit his ass already suspects something anyway because he keeps calling me. I've been giving him the fuck you button, ignoring his calls. Look, my phone is lit right now from all of the texts and voicemails," I explained laughing as I held my cell up for Honestii to read the screen.

"All I can say is that your ass is crazy as fuck, but I gotcha back no matter what you are doing."

"This is what we do Sis, because you know I got ya back too," I promised hugging my sister.

'From now on niggas will know how we're coming...'

Honestii

Soon as Khouri and I finished drinking and talking about hitting our next big lick, I regretted it. I was already trying to find a way out of it. The last thing we needed to do was rob someone, especially with a fucking gun. She knew how I felt about that shit.

I just let her go right ahead on and think I was down. I didn't want to burst her bubble; at least not until I had a plan to crush hers.

"Aight, I'm about to go to my room and lay down. A bitch's head is spinning," I told Khouri as I retreated to my room.

Right when I got inside and plopped down onto my bed, Marlon rang my phone reminding me about our lunch date. Instead of telling him I was drunk, I gave him the excuse that I wasn't feeling well.

"That's too bad," he sighed. "I guess that means you'll have to miss out on what I had for you."

My curiosity escalated right away, and I couldn't stop the words from flowing out of my mouth. "What, what did you have for me?"

"Never mind," he teased before telling me that he was on his way over.

We hung up and I tried to rush my ass through some water to help sober me up. Shit, it was before noon and I should have been ashamed of myself for getting so shit faced that damn early.

"Honestii, your bae is here! What the hell are you doing?" Khouri yelled through my locked door what seemed like fifteen minutes later.

"I'm coming damn!" I shouted back as I struggled to get into my jeans.

Shit, a bitch could barely breathe but I still had to rock them though. They were so fucking cute.

I slid my backless black tank on and slipped into a pair of multicolored heels. I half ass pinned my hair up and threw some shades on.

"Baby are you okay?" He questioned when I walked into the living room and nearly bumped into the end table. "Maybe if you take those dark glasses off..."

"No. Maybe if she didn't have those six shots," Khouri blurted out with a laugh before leaving the room.

So much for trying to hide the shit, ugh! I swear my sister was a fucking buster.

"Are you sure you wanna go out bae?" He asked as he helped me onto the sofa.

"I'm okay," I lied easing my sunglasses onto the top of my head.

Marlon sat down and scooted close to me before placing his arm around my shoulder. "Why were you drinking this early? Is something going on?"

"Honestii!" Khouri shouted from her bedroom.

The scream was so loud that it had me jumping up from my seat. I ran in there to see what was wrong and ignored the hell out of Marlon.

"What the hell?" I smirked looking at my sister sitting there on her bed with her arms folded.

She was pouting and holding the phone in the air. When she hit the speaker, I almost choked.

"Can somebody please pick me up from the airport?" I heard Paula ask with a little attitude.

"Why are you just now calling me?" Honestii snapped as she slid her shoes on.

My sister hit the mute button right in the middle of Paula talking. "Shit, you are going with me! I'm not gonna be stuck with this..."

"Hush, that's our blood! Just go get her," I replied turning up my lip. "I'm about to leave with Marlon."

"Ooooo, I swear I'm paying yo ass back Honestii!" Khouri threatened with a shake of her fist. "You better be back in a couple of hours because I'm not about to be babysitting her ass!"

"Babysit? That bitch is older than us!"

"Then why don't she get a rental car?"

"I don't know but get on the phone and tell her you're on your way. I'll be back in a few. I won't be gone too long."

Khouri rolled her eyes and told Paula that she was coming to get her. I knew she didn't want to go because she was still mad about the last time our cousin came.

Paula was our mothers' dead older brothers' daughter. The last time she came to visit we were teenagers. She is a few years older than us and thought she knew everything. We kind of ignored that but we couldn't let that shit slide when we caught her fucking Khouri's boyfriend after she helped us sneak him in.

I guess I would be salty too. Trust, I was going to watch her ass.

Shaking the memories, I joined Marlon back in the living room. He was standing there with a concerned expression.

"Is everything cool?" he questioned drawing me into his arms.

"Yeah bae," I answered as I pulled him towards the door. "That was just our cousin on the phone saying that she was in town. Khouri is going to get her from the airport so we can go."

Marlon clinched my hand and heaved me to him so that he could steal a kiss before we left. I welcomed it happily.

"So, what's my surprise?" I wasted no time asking.

"You'll see," he answered with a sneaky grin. "I have the next five days off work. Each one of those days I will give you a surprise."

"What do you mean?" I inquired feeling a bit confused. "So, I only get part of a gift? That's about fucked up."

"No, Honestii," Marlon laughed. "This is my first day off, so I'll start with a small gift. They will get bigger each day."

My heart raced with anticipation as I thought about the days to come. I had a bunch of questions.

Every time I asked him where we were going. He changed the subject each time with a joke. I was about to lose it until we drove up to a perfume emporium.

"You didn't have to bring me here to get me some perfume baby. You could have just gone to the mall and smelled a few fragrances until you found something that you liked," I explained still feeling excited that he would bring me with him to buy my gift.

"Well, it's gonna be a little more than that baby," he replied with a smile and came around and helped me out the car. "I signed us up to make our own perfume and cologne. We will get to pick and mix the fragrances ourselves and have them bottled and named. You can do one for me while I hook you up."

"What!" I exclaimed as I grabbed him and kissed his lips. "This is so sweet baby!"

"This is just the beginning Honestii. By day five I expect to have you speechless and in love."

I couldn't help but feel special. No one had ever done anything so sweet for me. It was truly a day to remember...

When we got inside, a woman took Marlon off while a man came and escorted me to a small lab. There were so many scents to choose from it took me over an hour to complete my cologne and pick my bottle. That wasn't as hard as it was to select a name for it.

I sat there thinking for ten more minutes before it came to me...'Estacio'. I don't know, but it just sounded exotic.

While the guy put the final touches on my bottle, I returned Marlon's text message. He had been trying to contact me for the past half hour.

"Okay, here you go. If you would like to order anymore bottles, we have your order saved on file."

"Oh, that's great!" I responded with a big smile. "Thank you so much!"

"You are very welcome ma'am and very lucky that your boyfriend brought you here. Not too many men do that for their women."

I blushed as the guy handed me the cologne. I hurried to examine it before he placed it into an exquisite gold box. I couldn't believe how it turned out. It truly looked professional.

After thanking the man once again, I grabbed my purse then headed out to the lobby. I knew my man was waiting on me.

"What took you so long?" He teased as we exchanged gifts.

I paid no attention to his reaction. I was too busy crying after I saw mine... *'Loving Honestii'*.

The shit was so fucking sweet...

Khouri

I could have killed Honestii for sticking me with picking Paula's snooty ass up by myself. I knew it was petty, but I still couldn't stomach her ass for sleeping with my boyfriend. Hell, I hadn't even fucked him!

As I pulled behind a taxicab at the front of the airport, I saw Paula standing there with her hand on her hip and much attitude. I rolled my eyes and blew the horn.

"Ugh, I can't stand this bitch," I huffed popping the trunk.

I sat my happy ass right in my seat and waited for her to load her own damn bags. I was not a valet or bellhop and she needed to know that shit from jump.

"So where are you staying?" I spit out before thinking.

"Damn girl, how have you been? Paula asked hastily.

"I've been doing well... you know living life to the fullest," I sarcastically replied. "I asked where you were staying because there are some nice hotels out here. I didn't want to get out the way before you told me."

Yes, I was trying to get rid of her ass. I didn't have time to babysit her. She was grown. Nor did I want this trick around either one of my niggas.

"Well my funds are low, so I was hoping that I could stay with you and Honestii for a few days."

There was no way in hell that I wanted her staying nowhere near me and my men! Did she forget what happened the last time I let her near my man?

I had to swallow the lump that had formed in my throat before I replied. If I didn't, I knew the wrong shit was likely to come out.

"I guess that will be fine Paula, long as you're not still into fucking folks' boyfriends."

Oops, too late...

"Oh, I know you're not still mad at me behind that. I was young and dumb then. I'm a grown ass woman now and I would never do anything like that to you again," she giggled.

That bitch had the nerve to think that shit was fucking funny. Shit, I was as serious as a heart attack.

'I should slap the taste out of her mouth.'

Paula tried making small talk throughout the thirty-five-minute drive back to the house, but I kept one wording her ass. I was still salty for having to pick her ass up and now I was stuck hosting her! Oh, yeah, I was beyond livid.

"So, what are you doing out this way?" I asked trying to determine how long Paula really planned on staying. There was no way her lying ass was giving me the full story. I had to try to pry it out of her.

"I came to find me a place. Well, I have a few appointments in the morning to look at some properties. New York is too damn expensive, and I figured that I would come back out here since all of my family is here."

I didn't quite have a response for her. I just nodded my head.

When we pulled into the driveway, Honestii came flying out with Marlon on her heels. The smile on her face said it all.

"Sissy, look what my baby made for me," she said practically shoving the perfume into my face.

I squirted the fragrance on my wrist, and at first it caused me to sneeze, but the smell of it was breathtaking. It was nice and subtle with a fresh scent.

"Aww, this is so sweet. I need to go make me some," I joked while I low-key wished someone would do something half as nice for me.

"You definitely should Sis."

At that time Paula hopped out that car and headed over to embrace Honestii. Honestly, I had forgotten all about her, for a brief second...

"Oh, my goodness, you've grown up to be so beautiful Honestii!" She screamed with her phony ass. Ugh, then she had the nerve to sweat Marlon too; just thirsty!

"Who is this handsome 'brotha?" She inquired with a flirtatious smile and a twist of her thick ass hips.

"Hey girl, thank you, and this is my boyfriend Marlon."

"Nice to meet you," he said extending his hand.

After they were introduced Marlon grabbed her bags and we all went into the house. Shit had that been me, Paula would have got her own damn bags.

"Come on Paula, let me show you where you're sleeping," Honestii offered while ushering her to the back.

I let my sister do all the work while I went in the kitchen and poured a glass of wine. That was the only thing that was going to help me through the day if I had to be around my annoying ass cousin.

Example, soon as he got settled in, she came out hollering that she was hungry. "What you in here cooking?"

"I'm drinking boo, not cooking," I smirked. "Feel free to cook whatever."

"Damn cuz, I'm jet lagged like shit. I really don't feel like cooking."

With no further discussion, I called out to order some Chinese because my ass wasn't cooking a damn thing. That was one thing I wasn't going to do, play Molly the fucking Maid!

While we waited for our food, Ruga came over with drinks, and we played spades. He had no idea that our cousin was in and Lord knew that I wanted to avoid the whole meet and greet session. I had serious trust issues when it came to her ass.

Looking down at my finger reminded me that I should have been secure in my fake ass relationship with Ruga. Worse than that, my stupid ass was engaged to him no less. Man, this shit is too funny to me.

The game I was playing with him had me so wrapped up that I was starting to believe it was real. I needed to snap myself up out of it.

Paula quickly assisted me by running her mouth. She just found shit to talk about so the attention could be on her.

"Y'all have such a nice place. I just hope that I can find something just as nice."

"Don't worry, you will cuz," Honestii announced.

"How long are you in town for?" Ruga asked as he smacked his card to the table.

I quickly shot his ass a look of disapproval. He just stared at me in confusion.

"I don't know yet, but for now three days. I might stay longer though."

'DING, DONG'

Just then our food arrived cutting their little conversation short. I knew that I had to get my emotions in check before I flew out the mouth sideways.

"How long have y'all been dating?" Paula pried.

I just looked over to Ruga. Stupid me for thinking the nigga was going to speak up first!

"We're actually engaged," I answered flashing my ring along with a big ass grin, right after frowning at Ruga.

"Oh shit, that's a nice ring, and here I thought it was just costume jewelry," Paula said jokingly.

Honestii and Marlon had stopped playing the game and looked at me. My sisters' eyes begged me not to go there, so I gave her ass a pass.

"No boo, this is the real deal, all thanks to my baby," I said leaning over kissing Ruga's soft lips.

"Well congratulations, you'll be the first one of the cousins to get married."

I gave her ass a tight grin and a dry ass thank you before Ruga and I went up to my bedroom. I didn't have time for her rude ass remarks.

"Baby, why did you give me that look when I asked your cousin how long she was staying?"

"It's a long story baby, and it isn't worth telling."

"Khouri, I could cut the tension between y'all with a knife. Something is wrong with that picture," he probed.

Taking a deep breath, I began telling Ruga what had previously happened with Paula and my ex-boyfriend, but I was interrupted mid-way through by the chime of the doorbell once again.

'DING, DONG'

"Y'all expecting company?" Paula asked.

"No, I'm not, so it's probably someone for Khouri or a Jehovah Witness. You know they do that door-to-door preaching stuff. They come by here at least a couple of times a month." Honestii laughed.

"Hey Khouri," Paula called out interrupting my story. I tried to ignore her, but she hollered out again within seconds.

"Khouri, you have a visitor!" She yelled.

When I got to the top of the stairs my heart dropped... it was Nahmir's ass. Baby, when I tell you my fucking legs were jelly. I thought I was gonna die right there.

I knew dodging him would finally make him chase me. I just didn't think that he would just show up without calling, especially when I had company. I swear he must have gotten a bad vibe or something because he had never done that before.

Checking behind me, I made sure Ruga wasn't following me before I went to see what Nahmir wanted. It had to be something.

I just prayed it was what I wanted to hear. What I needed to hear...

Honestii

It was way too late for me to stop Nahmir from fully entering the house. Hell, Paula had already opened the door and invited him in.

Marlon looked at me and I shrugged. "What?"

"Is Khouri still fuckin' with that nigga too?"

"No, but that's who has her heart. She just hasn't gotten him to act right yet," I answered truthfully. "When she does, I guess they'll be together."

He shook his head and waited for the outcome of the situation at hand. I just prayed that it didn't get ugly.

"Here she comes," I whispered as we watched her near us. Her face looked drained of all blood flow. She looked shook and that wasn't a look I was used to seeing my sister wear.

Feeling the tension right away, I got up and eased to my bedroom to retrieve my Taser. I wasn't sure if I would need it, but it was better to be safe than sorry because lord knows, I had no idea what type time he was on.

When I came back into the family room, this nigga was beginning to question my sister. He wanted to know why she hadn't called him, and some more shit.

"Well, we hadn't been seeing eye to eye, so I thought we needed a break," Khouri stuttered.

"A break? When the fuck was you gonna tell me?" he barked.

"Khouri?"

Suddenly Ruga began yelling out for my sister. Her face turned red as a beat as she just stood there without responding.

"Yeah," she replied with a shaky voice.

"Who the fuck is that?" Nahmir quizzed bringing his body to full attention.

"Baby could you bring me a bottled water when you come back up here please?" Ruga yelled out.

"Yeah, give me a minute," she hollered back.

"Nah, let's go take him that shit right now," Nahmir suggested as he walked in my sister's personal space.

"Hey, Slim please don't bring no mess up in here," I warned with one raised brow as I entered the room.

I prayed that was enough to let him know that I wouldn't hesitate to shoot a jolt of electricity in his ass. He knew that we both had weapons so he should have known better to test us.

"Don't worry, I'm not Honestii." He smirked. "The mess was already here!"

Suddenly him and my sister began going back and forth arguing. Once their tone elevated, Ruga came running down the stairs.

"What the fuck is going on?" Ruga rushed in front of my sister and got in Nahmir's face. "We got a problem nigga?"

Khouri went to grab Ruga and Nahmir snatched her hand and stared at the ring. "Ain't this a bitch?"

"Nigga this is my girl! I don't know what y'all had before, but all that shit is dead my guy!"

"Yeah, I see that shit now," Nahmir huffed in defeat.

I felt so sorry for him, but I didn't want to get in the middle of it. Khouri knew she was in love with that man. I didn't understand why she just wouldn't come clean about her feelings.

"I should just fuck you up!" Nahmir threatened as he lunged towards Khouri. "You lucky I don't hit women, or you would be touching everything up in here right now!"

Ruga bucked up at the wrong time. Soon as he did, Nahmir knocked him the fuck out. I swear I wanted to laugh but I couldn't.

"Damn, why did you do that?" Paula screamed hysterically as she rushed over to Ruga on the floor. "Somebody help him!"

Khouri gave Nahmir the look of death then shook her head. "Leave, please…"

"I'm gone, but we're gonna talk. This shit ain't over!"

The loud slam of the door snapped Ruga to attention. My sister hurried back over to him and shoved Paula out of the way. "I got this."

"Then why the hell did you take so long? The fuck."

"Paula, stay out of it and let Khouri handle it!"

Our cousin hurried up and got her ass up off the floor and went to pour her another drink. "Fuck it, I'm going to sleep!"

"That sounds like a damn good idea," Honestii spoke.

Within seconds everyone had cleared the room, leaving me and Marlon sitting there all alone. I almost forgot he was there.

He looked at me and we both start laughing. The shit was funny...

"I hope we don't ever have to go through no shit like that baby," he stated and kissed my cheek.

"Not on my part we won't," I teased. "You better not have no skeletons bae!"

"Naw, I cut off all my fans once we got serious," he teased as he took me into an embrace.

"Oh, so you are saying that you had bitches before me huh?" I asked jealously.

"You know I'm playing baby. I've never been that type. One woman is hard enough to have. I couldn't imagine dealing with two!"

"Oh, so I'm difficult?" I inquired with a curious expression.

"No, not at all baby," he smiled. "You're not easy either. You are somewhere in between and that's perfect."

"Aw, you're so sweet," I whispered and gave his lips a peck.

"I love you Honestii," he replied with a big grin. "I'm gonna show you every day."

I just melted into his arms thinking about my second gift that he planned on giving me the following day. I couldn't wait...

Khouri

After I snatched up the ice pack out of the freezer, I went upstairs to put it on Ruga's eye. Before I closed the door, I heard my sister and Marlon ass laughing about the messy ass bullshit that had just taken place.

"What the fuck was that? I didn't know you had a thing going on with that nigga, Khouri."

"I'm sorry baby, but since me and you started kicking it, I haven't seen him."

"Naw, that shit don't even sound right ma. If that was the case, then why was that nigga all vexed when he saw me?"

"Man, I don't know why he ain't got the hint yet. I haven't even spoke to him in months," I lied.

"How long was y'all live?" Ruga probed.

"We were together for a few years and he cheated on me, so I cut his ass."

"Are you talking about cutting him off or your feelings off because it seems like you still feeling that nigga?"

"Stop with all that shit! I just told you what it was!" I insisted with an attitude.

"Khouri, I don't give a fuck about what you're saying right now. You should have made it clear to that nigga! You can't just stop seeing a man and not let him know when it's officially over! Come on baby, you're not dumb."

"I know that I should have let him know, but I really thought that he would have caught on after I stopped answering his calls and text messages."

"I hate to say it, but that nigga is gonna catch some hot shit if he ever come at me like that again. He caught me slippin' this time, but you can bet ya ass it won't happen again!" He barked.

While Ruga ranted, my mind raced with so many thoughts. I really wanted to nut the fuck up on Nahmir for the stunt he pulled, but I had to put the shoe on the other foot, and in that case... I would have flipped out too. As for Ruga, I think his ego was more hurt than anything.

"Look baby, I'm very sorry. That shit won't happen again, and I will make sure his ass knows that what we had is history," I lied. Nahmir was my heart and now that he showed me, he cared, I couldn't wait to talk to him. I just had to take care of the matter at hand first; Ruga.

I did my best to reassure him that I was his. That had to be done in order to keep my plan intact.

I knew both of their capabilities and trust me it wasn't going to be a good outcome if things weren't handled right away. I didn't want that to happen.

"I love you baby," I told Ruga letting that lie slip easily out of my mouth. Don't judge me, I still needed to keep this nigga at arm's length.

From there we started drinking and an hour later I was horny but Ruga was not the one. I wasn't about to fuck his ass. I was completely satisfied by Nahmir in that department. Even though we hadn't done shit in what seemed like forever.

"Yeah just a lil' more time and it will all be over," I thought right before I drifted off to sleep.

****

The next morning, I waited until Ruga left then I went downstairs and made me a mimosa. Upon passing my sister's bedroom, I heard her and Marlon fucking again. The graphic image that popped into my head gave me chills then turned my stomach. Lord who wanted to think of their little sister getting dicked down. Now I knew how she must have felt when Nahmir would come over and we would be in the room fucking up the headboard.

After deleting the sickening visual that disturbed my mental, I fixed myself a bagel. Then I went back to my bedroom to see what I could find on TV.

Several moments passed by and I was still browsing through the channels. I couldn't find shit, so I gave up and set the remote down on the bed beside me with the sounds of 'Boys in The Hood' playing in the background.

Taking a deep breath, I closed my eyes as I contemplated on making that awkward call to Nahmir. I slowly dialed his number, and long pressed the last digit.

"What!" He yelled.

"Damn you don't have to holler at me nigga! I'm calling to talk to you, like you asked.

"Man, I'm not talking to you over no fuckin' phone! Get to my spot in thirty," he huffed disconnecting my call.

Shit, I knew that I didn't need to go over there and start more confusion, but I desperately wanted to get that shit over and done with. I felt I had no choice.

I threw on some sweats and an old t-shirt and headed out the door. I stopped by Honestii room on the way out.

'KNOCK, KNOCK'

"I'll be back Sis," I said walking off.

"I love you!" She shouted back.

"Love you too!"

I went out and got in my car. I was nervous to see him after the shit with Ruga, so I took my time driving over there.

By the time I arrived at his crib, I had beads of sweat rolling down my forehead and the palms of my hands sweated profusely. He was sitting on the front porch waiting for my ass.

He flicked his Newport when I put my car in park. Again, I took a deep breath and I then exited the car.

Before I could get out my ride good enough, Nahmir was on my ass.

"What the fuck is this shit Khouri?" He shouted grabbing my left hand.

'Fuck!' I silently cursed myself. In a rush I forgot to take my ring off. Yeah, he had seen it the night before, but maybe I could have played it off. Now my ass was cold busted.

"Slim, I can explain..."

"Fuck that Khouri, this is an engagement ring! You fuckin' with this nigga like that?" He questioned me with tear filled eyes.

I was honestly lost for words. I truly loved Nahmir. I mean fuck, we had been through a lot of shit together. On the other hand, Ruga was my mark and now I had the keys and access to his wealth I was about to get him. I just wasn't sure about letting this nigga in on it. I didn't think he would understand.

"Slim, I really didn't mean to hurt you or anything like that, but you and I haven't been seeing eye to eye in a long time. Maybe we should just..."

"Come in the house," he ushered me. "Look, I'm not letting you go Khouri, and you're not marrying his ass. We are forever," he said pulling me into a kiss.

"No Slim, I can't do this anymore. Your ass don't even want a commitment that's real. All you wanna do is throw these parties and get money or go out and fuck random bitches. I'm not with that. That shit gets old after a while."

"Baby I promise if you give me another chance, I will change the game and settle down with you, on my mama."

"I have so much love for you, but I can't. I have to think about this thing with Ruga…"

Ugh, it was eating me up inside. I wanted badly to tell him that Ruga was just money in my eyes, but then he would want in on it and that wasn't about to go down like that.

"Fuck that nigga! Come here!"

Nahmir snatched me up and lifted me onto the pool table. His ass was wasting no time! He immediately tore my sweats off and began to devour my sweet juices that flowed freely.

Instead of fighting him off me, I wrapped my legs around his shoulders and relaxed my hips. Some oral sex was way overdue, and I took full advantage one his tongue as it caressed my fat juicy pussy before he latched onto my clit. That was when I humped upwards and held onto Nahmir until I exploded the first time. He licked every drop up with a long slurp.

"Ooooooooooo," I sang out becoming more aroused. I wanted him and he knew it. Fuck! I needed that.

"Come here girl," he whispered pulling me closer, as he looked into my eyes with love mixed with lust.

"Ahh, yes baby," I moaned as he slid his thick long tongue into my pussy while teasing my G-spot. That caused him to go deeper.

"My fucking goodness!" I yelled as I pushed his head further into my wetness.

This went on for the next twenty minutes. That was right after Nahmir made me explode two more times. He then helped me sit up and kissed me deeply with his juicy lips.

Hopping up off the pool table, I allowed him to position me so he could hit it from the back. I knew that he had to have missed me by his aggressiveness. I mean that nigga was beating it up something fierce. Shit, before it was all over, he had my ass yelping like a wounded animal.

"Fuck Khouri, you feel so fuckin' good! I don't want nobody but you baby!"

No more needed to be said. Those were just the right words to cause my juices to come flowing out of me like an erupted volcano.

My thick liquid eased down his balls and slowly dripped onto his leg. Once he felt me leaking all over him, he busted what felt like a fucking bucket of water being splashed up inside of me. *Thanks to you God, for inventing birth control pills. I laughed inward.*

"Damn baby," he panted as he finally released the tight grip, he had on me.

When he backed all the way up, I saw that his dick was still standing at attention. That along with the look in his eyes let me know that he was searching for round two. Yes, I gave my man just what he wanted.

I was no mo' good after that...

Honestii

The past four days had been mind-blowing. I mean sure I got gifts before, but the ones that Marlon had been laying on me were thoughtful and personal. They had me feeling loved, and I mean like I never had before.

The perfume was a beautiful gesture and I kept the bottle on my dresser to remind me every day that Marlon was hi loving me. It made me feel special, but not like the gift I received on the second day.

Do you know that he really took me to a designer and had an outfit made especially for me? I got to have it made anyway I wanted, and that shit was dope! It was all black and accentuated my shape beautifully.

By day three, I was blown away. Marlon shocked me. Although his gift wasn't one for me, the meaning behind it meant the world though.

That day he led me over to the Baptist Church that had gotten burned down a few weeks prior. I was confused as we walked over to a small gathering. The preacher said a few words and then did a dedication on rebuilding the sanctuary.

Let me tell you, my mouth fell wide open when they thanked me and Marlon for our ten-thousand-dollar donation. They had our names engraved in a brick and everything. Afterwards several families came and thanked us. Some were even crying. That was an incredible feeling for real...

Okay, now the following day was the fourth day and I was anxious as hell. I was bright eyed and ready to go by seven in the morning. Marlon didn't arrive until nine, so I had to wait.

When he finally managed to get there, he made me drive my car and I had to follow him. The whole way there I was fidgeting and wondering where the hell we were going. The only thing I could think of was a new car. Although I had a new whip. Well, it was new to me, but a brand spanking new one would be a wonderful surprise.

How wrong I was! My guess was totally off.

"A fucking garage?" I huffed as we pulled into this little rinky dink ass auto shop.

'To think I was gonna get a new car.'

I got out and forced a smile as we walked into the office together. It was surprisingly nice inside and had a lot of new gadgets displayed.

"Why are we here?" I quizzed raising a brow.

"We're gonna 'pimp yo ride'!" He laughed as the guy took me to the computer to do a questionnaire. They wanted to know everything from my favorite color to my favorite song.

"It's gonna be a minute," the worker said causing Marlon to turn to me.

"Whatcha wanna get into?" he asked. "This may take all day."

"I don't know. Let's just go out to the boulevard and see what's poppin," I laughed as we held hands and began our day out.

While we waited, we wound up shopping, site seeing and eating twice. It wasn't until late that night when we went back to get my little Honda Accord.

Man, when I saw that shit I screamed so much and so damn loud that I gave myself a sore throat. Y'all! That shit was dope as fuck! They painted it was all black and everything was accented with gold trim. It was so elegant.

The interior was all decked out with every gadget available. There were things like a water dispenser, Pandora radio, a small pop out vanity with all types of makeup and it even had a built-in cooler. The extras were endless...

"Let me let you go home because we have a big day ahead of us tomorrow," Marlon sighed as we parted our ways at the garage.

"Okay baby, I can't wait," I smiled before kissing him deeply. "I can't thank you enough for what you've already done for me. You've made me the happiest girl in town." Now, I was livid that he wasn't coming back home with me, but I wanted that last gift more.

"Oh, hold that thought baby," Myles laughed as he ushered me into my newly 'pimped out' ride. He closed the door without allowing me to respond.

I can only imagine...

****

Now there we were on day five and I was sweating bullets. I mean my ass was nervous when he picked me up looking extra scrumptious. He was not only fine as hell, he smelled delicious. I didn't hesitate to tell him either.

"Oh, thank you," He laughed as we drove along on our last mysterious date.

"I'm a little nervous," I admitted as I held on to his right hand as he clinched the steering wheel with his left.

I must have questioned him all the way up until we parked in front of a large office building that was located downtown. This time I had no idea what he was up to, so I really started wondering out loud.

"Why are you tripping?" He asked laughing as he clasped my palm and led me inside the huge structure.

"I'm not," I lied as we approached the elevators to the tenth floor. When we got off, we turned to the left and stopped in front of a large glass window with all types of stones and metals on display.

"What is this place?" I asked as I looked down at my clothes.

I was feeling way over dressed and uncomfortable, but I went along with it.

"Come on. This will be fun," he replied as he tried to convince as we stepped through the door.

We were greeted by a small man holding a tray with champagne flutes. "Hello sir, Manuel is expecting you, and his wife Sara will be helping the Mrs."

"Hmmm, the Mrs. huh?" I joked finding it rather amusing.

Taking a seat, both Marlon and I enjoyed a couple of glasses of bubbly. "So, what are we going to do here? Is this a masseuse or something?"

"No," Marlon laughed. "Today we are going to make each other gifts made of precious stones and metal. I thought that this was a good idea because it will last forever…"

"Are you ready?" Manuel and his wife interrupted.

Before Marlon could finish, Sara was whisking me off to a private room to make my selections. It was simple because I knew about nothing but diamonds and gold.

"I want to make a medallion that he can wear on his chain." I requested. "I want it round, and in the middle spelled in diamonds I want 'M & H'.

"What color diamonds would you like?"

"Oh, they come in different colors?" I blurted out then covered my mouth.

Sara showed me all the selections they had there, and I knew right away that I wanted the blue ones. That was Marlon's favorite color.

Once she took my order, she instructed me to wait in the office lobby. I thanked her and left the room.

"You're done already?" Bae asked as I entered the lobby where he was waiting on me. He then led me out of the office and downstairs to leave the building.

"Yes, that was different," I smiled wondering what we were about to do for the rest of the day while we waited. "What's up now?"

"I thought since you were all dressed up, looking all nice and shit we would go somewhere fancy and have brunch since it is Sunday."

"Okay, I'm still feeling the champagne, but I sure could eat," I grinned as I rubbed my stomach.

We stepped out into the beautiful sunshine. I slid my sunglasses down over my eyes and watched the small hummingbirds that seemed to be playing tag.

"Let me see…" Marlon chanted as he pulled up some information on his cell. "There's a jazz brunch over at the Hilton. That's just a few blocks over. You wanna walk?"

I nodded and we marched off hand in hand.

"What did you make?" I questioned as we strolled along the sidewalk. I couldn't help myself.

"Huh?"

"What did you make at the jewelers?" I repeated. "I hope I didn't go overboard with mine, but Sara said I didn't have a spending limit."

Marlon clinched my hand tighter and then stopped in his tracks. Looking down at me, he gave me a serious expression.

"What?" I shrugged. "That's what she told me."

"Nah, I'm just messing with you, bae. I'm sure whatever it is I'm going to love it."

"Yes, because I made it from my heart," I replied stretching the truth because honestly, I didn't know what the hell I was doing.

"I know you did," he smiled as we made it to the Hilton.

"Now what did you make me?" I asked anxiously.

Man, I tell you. Marlon avoided that question all the way through brunch.

Since I saw that he wasn't budging, I began badgering him about what we were going to do next.

Glancing down at his watch, Marlon suggested we catch a movie. I was thinking something totally different. He quickly got the hint when he looked at me giving him the *'come fuck me'* eyes.

"Your house or mine?" he whispered as we approached his car.

Without a second thought, I said my house. It was a lot closer than his place was.

When we got there, I had to go to the bathroom bad as hell. All that champagne and orange juice was working a number on my bladder.

Struggling with my keys, I unlocked the door and we entered the living room. "You can wait right here, and I'll be right back."

I rushed to the bathroom inside my room and freshened up and picked up the clothes that were lying around. I didn't want to bring Marlon in there with my room looking all tore up and shit.

After tidying up a bit, I walked down the hallway, towards the front. That was when I heard Paula's voice. She was all giggling and shit.

"Damn, you think you wanna put some clothes on cuz?" I smirked as I checked her out.

Paula was wearing a piece of tank top and some shorts cut so high that her ass cheeks were hanging out. I had to shake my head in disgust.

"What the hell you mean by that?" She snapped and twirled around so fast that one of her 'Double D' titties popped out. It came out just far enough that you could see her pierced nipple.

"Damn!" Marlon laughed putting his fist up to his mouth and raising one leg.

Mustering up the dirtiest look I could, I directed it towards my man's disrespectful ass. I swear I could have fucked his ass up right there on the spot!

"Let's go! We can just go to your place." I fussed while snatching up my handbag and keys.

Marlon didn't say shit once I spoke my peace and headed for the door. He just got his ass up and followed me outside.

Rushing over to my door, he opened it up. Yes, it was a nice gesture, but his timing was all off. It was too late. I was already in my bag.

After we drove off and got a few blocks down the road, I called Khouri. I just had to vent about Paula trifling ass.

"What's up Sis? How was day five boo?" My sister sang.

"Good, thanks, but anyway, I just left the house, and do you know that Paula is there prancing around in next to nothing?" I complained bypassing a summary of my last surprise date. "You know I walked in with Marlon, so I wasn't happy at all."

"No worries Sis," Khouri assured. "I'll be pulling up to the house in the next hour, so I'll check her ass then. I swear I can't stand a thirsty bitch!"

We hung up and I set the phone on my thigh. Upon rising back up, I snuck a peek at Marlon. He caught me.

"My fault," he whispered with a half-ass admission of guilt before glancing back at the road.

"It's okay," I lied. That shit still had me heated.

'His ass just better be making it up to me by putting a bomb sex session on me then topping it off with a real apology.'

I pouted silently but then smiled just knowing that Marlon would provide me with just what I needed. That thought alone brought warmth to my heart and a throb in my panties...

Without checking with me first, Marlon took me to his house. I didn't object. Instead I followed him right on inside and let him love me like he said he would. I held him to every bit of his promise the moment we stepped inside of his bedroom.

Beginning with my dress, he slid it up over my head while unfastening my front clasped bra. The moment my breasts were free, he latched onto one as he gently massaged the other.

"Mmmmm," I moaned as I helped him undress. He managed to get completely nude without letting loose of my left nipple. He only released it momentarily to chant the magical phrase that I hadn't been able to repeat back yet,

"I love you." I mean don't get me wrong, I said it when I felt like it, but during sex, I just couldn't. Shit, we all know that anyone says whatever while fucking, making love or whatever you call it.

There were no more words after that; only passionate groans. In the end, we both were totally satisfied. That was when I got my heartfelt apology. It was all I wanted...

****

Hours later, we finally got up out of Marlon bed and went to the jewelers to pick up our gifts. I couldn't wait to see what Marlon had created for me.

"Here you go," I smiled as I gave him the large box.

I was so damn excited for him to see his gift that I almost forgot about getting mine. "Open it!"

Marlon took the gift from my hand and removed the lid. "What? This shit right here is dope, baby!"

"You like it?"

"I fuckin' love this shit right here!" Marlon yelled out and held it closer so he could take a better look at it.

"So, I take it that means it's a good thing, huh?"

"Yeah, it's a great thing," Marlon grinned as he slid the chain with the medallion over his head and let it rest on his chest.

"My turn now!" I shouted like a kid.

Marlon got the box from his jacket and handed it to me. "Wait," he chanted as he held it back from me.

"What?" I asked feeling confused.

"I love you," Marlon spoke so sincerely that it made me tear up. I couldn't stop the tears if I wanted to.

"I love you too," I whispered barely able to spit it out.

Marlon let go of me and stood back then stared me down with tears as well.

Marlon took me into his strong arms and held me tightly, picked me up then kissed me until I couldn't breathe. When he released me, he stood back and held out the box. I didn't have it out of his hand good before I popped the lid off and eyed the most gorgeous two-tiered wedding set ever.

"It's so beautiful Marlon," I cried.

He held onto my left hand and kneeled right before me. He lifted his head up to me and asked...

"Will you do me the honor?"

"Hu, hu, huh?" I stuttered.

"Honestii, will you marry me?" He asked sincerely as he released a few tears as well.

"Yes, yes and hell yes baby!"

We were so wrapped up into one another that I didn't even remember anything else that happened that day. The only thing that was on my mind was planning a wedding.

I didn't know what was going on in my sister's crazy world, but Marlon and I were on the right path to spending the rest of our lives together. We were official. That was all I ever wanted.

'Once I get married, all the stealing has got to stop! I just hope my sister understands...'

Khouri

"Why is yo ass always causing conflict? Damn! Let's get this straight Paula. You should have been gone by now. You're a guest in our house and that half-naked shit ain't gonna fly. You need to keep clothes on yo ass before somebody gets hurt and it won't be my sister or me," I sharply told her before walking off.

"Whatever Khouri!" Paula yelled.

I didn't give two fucks about her little pissy ass. I meant what the fuck I said! She was going to get fucked up if that shit happened again. *On my mama.*

Nahmir had been blowing my phone up threatening me. He was pressuring me to break things off with Ruga after our last discussion. I couldn't though. I had gone through too much to back out now. I needed to hit my mark before I could do that. Nahmir would have to be patient.

If I had to, I would just tell him the truth. I at least owed him that much.

Yes, Nahmir and I had an understanding when it came to business. That was why it had been so hard to tell him what I had brewing. I knew that he would want to be a part of it but that couldn't happen because I had to get close to Ruga. Nahmir already made it clear that he didn't want that. To sum things up, I was in over my head, but I was about to handle it, especially now that Ruga was acting funny. You see in the past he never had any problem expressing his feelings. That was up until he found out about Nahmir.

Ever since then he had been a little quieter and laid back. He had been distancing himself from me. I figured his ego may have been crushed, so I gave him his space for the time being, but it wouldn't be for too long. Shit, I needed my money…

****

That day I chilled at the house and waited until the next night to do a pop-up visit on Ruga. I was finally about to lay it on real think and make him think I was deeply in love with him. It had been a longtime coming. He had been very patient with me, but it was all about timing. You see that night he was about to think he had my heart.

'Right before I take him for all he has.'

As I drove to his house in complete silence, my thoughts ran rapid. I knew that what I was about to do would forever change things. Not only was I about to deceive him, I was about to rob him blind.

'All I had do is set the trap.'

There was a pit in the bottom of my stomach that said something wasn't right, but I just wrote it off as my nerves and kept right on my mission. I wasn't about to let that little shit stop me.

"Where is he?" I whispered as I threw my car in park.

When I pulled up to Ruga's crib the lights were out, so I didn't think he was home. At first, I was going to turn back around, but then I decided against it. I just went ahead and waited on him. I needed to get him to trust me. I needed him all in.

With no hesitation, I used my key to let myself into the house. "Ruga!" I called his name upon entering, but there was no reply. My voice was already a little hoarse, so I didn't repeat myself.

As I stood at the bottom of the two-way staircase, I heard music playing from up in Ruga's bedroom. Since I knew that he always left Pandora on the 'Love Jams' station when he wasn't home, there was no need for me to climb all of those stairs.

Now when Ruga was home, he bumped nothing but hip-hop and always had it blasting. But, since Jill Scott was on and playing softly, I knew he couldn't be home. Just to make sure, I checked the garage.

On my way there, I could have sworn I heard some squeaking and knocking coming from up above the back hallway. When I became very still, the noises went away.

"Maybe those were my footsteps," I laughed to myself as I opened the door that led to the garage. "I must be trippin' for real!"

After cutting on the light, I saw right away that his favorite SUV was missing. I knew he had to be in the streets. That shit was the norm for him.

"I wonder when he's coming home." I spoke out loud as I peeked into the kitchen while I contemplated on dialing Ruga's cell.

Dismissing the thoughts temporarily, I eased on into the back of the pantry and went over to the alcohol shelves to draw out a fifth of Apple Cîroc. After coming out and grabbing a glass, I crept on over to the refrigerator to get a few cubes of ice.

Once my drink was perfect, I went into the den and stared out of the window for not even a full minute before I quickly became bored. I downed my drink and went back in the kitchen to refill my glass.

After that second double shot of Cîroc on the rocks, I didn't go back in the den. Instead, I headed straight upstairs to the bedroom to freshen up. I knew Ruga would be home soon, so I wanted to take a quick shower before he got there.

As I drew closer to the double doors of Ruga's sleeping quarters, I heard the faint sounds of a woman's whimpers. At first, I thought it was part of the song that was playing, but the nearer I got, the more I realized that it was coming from an actual person.

Taking in a deep breath as I cracked the slightly opened door, I looked inside. The sight immediately had me gasping for fucking air. That shit seriously had me tripping.

What the hell? I thought silently as my blood pressure rose to an all-time high.

After rubbing my eyes, I refocused my vision, but the live action was just the same. There was Paula bent over, bucking back like a horse, while Ruga fucked the shit out of her from behind.

My whole body went numb and I began to shake uncontrollably. Off pure instinct, I wanted to rush down to my car, grab the wop and shoot both of their asses' dead, but I had to be smart about my shit because I still had to get that bag. Now all I needed was a better plan.

Biting the bullet, I turned around and slowly crept back down the stairs, slid my shoes on, grabbed that bottle of Cîroc and beat the highway back to the crib. I wasn't dumb. I was going to use all that shit against both of 'em.

Fuck them! I shouted in my head as I pulled up at the house.

The second I got inside. Honestii was on my ass about my whole demeanor. I tried to hide my face so that she couldn't read my expressions, but she was all on me.

"What's the matter with you Sis?" She quizzed.

"Nothing, I just feel sick as hell. Where is Paula at tonight?"

I knew my sister wouldn't stand for no bullshit like that, so I had to play it off. I didn't want her to suspect a thing until I was ready to pull my rabbit out of the hat trick.

"I think she said she had a house to go look at. "Honestii explained before she shifted to an *'out of the blue'* question. "Are you pregnant KK?"

"Hell, nah girl. I rebuke the devil in the name of Jesus," I replied jokingly trying to hide my true feelings.

"Well, I made dinner. Come in here and try to eat something. Maybe it will make you feel better," Honestii whined.

"No Sis, I couldn't eat if I wanted to right now," I told her as I turned to go to my room.

"Well I will put a plate up for you then!" She yelled to me.

"Alright babes. Thank you," I replied.

"Maybe later Sis."

God it was killing me not to tell my little sister what I had witnessed. I didn't though because I knew her ass would flip the shits after something like that, and that was a no-no.

I had to be patient about it. To get those mother fuckers back was going to take some time. I had to use my head instead of my pride. At that moment it was fucking crushed.

Heading up to my bedroom, I had my bottle of alcohol in hand. I entered, closed myself in and took my first swig.

I drank more and more Cîroc while quietly crying my eyes out. I couldn't front, my feelings were truly hurt. Not only did I think I had Ruga in the palm of my hand, but he betrayed me.

As for Paula, I expected it out of her ass. In a sick way I was glad she crossed me again.

'This time I'll get her ass good.'

Silently I wondered if I had been that bad of a person to make people betray me. If it wasn't Nahmir, it was Ruga and Paula. I had truly had enough, and I was getting sick and tired of it, especially Ruga. He didn't have to get me back like that because of that bullshit with Nahmir. I would have had way more respect for Ruga if he just dumped me. That right there only angered me more.

"Damn, that's fucked up!" I complained as I continued to guzzle down the soothing alcohol.

I couldn't seem to shake the fact that I had gone over there to set my trap and instead walked into the biggest surprise of the year. Yeah, that shit hurt.

I guess I didn't know Ruga as well as I thought. Either that or he really didn't know how I got down; but Paula did. If she didn't remember, I was about to jog that dizzy bitch's memory. I wasn't the one to be played with.

Now just because that nigga did me dirty, don't think I was going to call off the engagement. I was about to work it for all that it was worth.

I refused to be sitting around looking stupid and not getting my funds while that whore Paula was collecting. No sir! I was just going to chuck the shit up to the game and focus on getting paid.

'Oh well, I guess I'm glad the shit happened just like it did. Now I don't feel so bad...'

Honestii

When Khouri came storming in the house, I knew something was wrong. Her whole demeanor was strange enough for me to question it.

After trying so hard to convince me that she wasn't feeling well, I let the shit go and continued to catch up on season one of 'Saint's and Sinners'. Yes, it was a *'Prime'* solo evening for me.

I was dressed in my two-piece San Francisco 49'ers pajamas because they were so damn comfortable. Plus, they were my favorite football team.

"Mmmmm, this is so good," I sang as I fucked up my bowl of Turkey Hill Cookies and Cream flavored ice cream.

I plopped back down on the sofa and covered up with my *'Boston Celtic'* throw blanket.

Grabbing the remote, I hit the 'pause' button and restarted the fourth episode of my show. Shit had been so hectic that I hadn't even told my sister that I was engaged, hell she hadn't even noticed either.

Right when it got to the good part, in came Paula. I looked up from the seventy-two-inch television and eyed her down. The devious smile that covered her face immediately sent a bad vibe through me.

"Hey lil' cousin," she grinned while coming to join me in the family room.

Paula plopped down on the sofa reeking of weed, sex and men's cologne. The combination was fucking up my nose and my stomach.

"Damn, you don't smell yourself?"

I sat up and frowned when she looked at me. She got right up and rolled her eyes.

"You know what? You and Khouri be trippin'. Y'all be treating me like y'all so much better than me. That's okay though. I have something in the works so I'm really sure that I will be up out of here real soon."

"How soon?" I asked anxiously.

"No later than next week. Who knows? If I work my magic just right it could be as early as tomorrow," she boasted then smirked. "Don't worry. I'm just as ready to get up out this muthafucka as you are ready for me to go. Believe that shit cuz!"

Paula didn't wait for a reply. She just pranced her stinking ass to the back. She was hopefully on her way to wash that funky ass. I couldn't get up and spray the Lysol fast enough.

Now that I had that broad and the funky smell out of my way, I kicked back and watched my show. As anxious as I was to see it, I could barely keep my eyes open for twenty minutes.

Sleep won the battle for a few hours, but after that I was right back up with Marlon on my mind. I needed to see him.

Picking up my cell, I dialed him up for a late-night creep. I guess he was thinking about me too because soon as he answered he told me that he was coming to see me.

"Where are you baby?" I whispered.

"I'm right down the street. Unlock the door," he instructed before disconnecting the call.

I was still tired, but I managed to get up and fulfill his request. Once I did, I stretched right on out and drew my blanket over my head.

It had to be about ten minutes later when I heard Marlon coming in. He came right to me, removed his shoes and climbed beside me on the extended wraparound sofa.

Cuddling close, he whispered that he loved me. I could smell the mint on his breath that was doing a poor job of masking the gas he smoked. It didn't bother me though. I was still just as turned on by his touch.

"Oooo, I want some babe," Marlon begged in a low tone. "Let's go to your room."

Whisking me off, he took me to the back, into the privacy of my bedroom and placed me gently on my back. Next, he began to undress me while kissing me along the way.

His lips were soft and felt so good against my skin. Every peck sent sensational bolts of pleasure throughout my body. I loved every second of it.

"I wanna taste you," he moaned as his kisses trailed from my breasts to my hot spot that was growing hotter by the second.

The minute he touched his tongue to my clit, I wrapped my thighs around his shoulders and thrust upwards. "Damn daddy!"

As the rhythm of my pumps increased in speed, I felt an orgasm coming. I just knew it was going to be a good one too, until...

"What the fuck you, doing?" I heard Khouri bark at Honestii's room during what looks to be a very private moment!"

I must have kicked Marlon off the end of the bed without thinking. I was so shocked by it all. Hell, I thought the damn door was closed.

While Marlon scrambled to get up, Paula tucked her tits back into her piece of shirt and got to stepping. It wasn't quick enough for Khouri though.

"Now keep your ass in your own fucking area!" My sister snapped as she mushed the back of Paula's head and made her stumble into the wall.

"See, you are so fucking lucky that we are blood because if not, I would be beating your ass right now!"

"Or getting your ass beat?" Khouri clowned as she entered Paula's arm reach.

I rushed out of my room to get between them. "Cut the shit out!"

I honestly didn't care if they got into a knockdown drag out fight. I just didn't want to hear that shit right then. Besides, it was seriously fucking up my private time with my nigga and I was getting pissed.

My sister went upstairs to her room and slammed the door. Then, Paula did the same. Now it was my turn.

"Damn, that shit was a little embarrassing," Marlon admitted as he rubbed the facial hair that was neatly trimmed around his mouth.

"No, it wasn't! Fuck them," I replied as I crawled seductively across the bed until I reached him.

"Yeah," he said in between the kisses he came and gave me. "You're just saying that shit because I was the one that got caught going down on you. Now if that would have been you sucking my dick, and someone came in, it would have been another story."

"Well, let me just see about that," I teased while unbuckling his pants and releasing the beast. "I'm about to get you ready to put it down on me. Lay back and relax while I service you now."

Marlon quickly obeyed and the shit was on. His started turning-up toes and all. My head skills were the best and I knew my man loved it...

Khouri

A couple of weeks had passed, and I still hadn't even mentioned to anyone what I had seen between Ruga and Paula's ass. Truth was I hardly cared anymore but my ego was still totally crushed. What kept me intact though was Nahmir. I kicked it with him every chance I got.

It was hard though, with Ruga constantly harassing me for sex. That was until I came up with the plan not to give him any until we got married. I was very sorry to say that it was going to be *'never'* when that happened.

As for Paula, I had been snapping on her every time I saw her ass. On top of that shit, Honestii was in my face every day asking me what was bothering me. As badly as I wanted to tell her I couldn't because she would not keep her mouth shut about that shit. I couldn't risk her blabbing. It would ruin my plan.

After a few weeks, there I was thinking that Ruga didn't even notice that I had been distant and different around him. How wrong was I? He began catering to me and all my needs. It was getting to the point that he didn't want to leave my side and when he did, he made sure to check in. The shit was crazy, but it was just what I needed to happen. He had to be feeling guilty about fucking Paula. I had been dropping little lugs ever since the shit took place.

"Let's get married this week," Ruga begged out of the blue.

He had been nagging me all day. If it wasn't about getting married, it was about fucking me. I swear that nigga was in my ear for a full hour. I did nothing but give him excuse after excuse why it couldn't happen so soon. Ruga wouldn't let up.

"Baby fuck all that red tape shit! If I marry you, I trust you. Now let's just go to the Justice of the Peace tomorrow. I just wanna be able to call you my wife. I'm tired of waiting," Ruga tried to convince.

"I really would like to have a church wedding Ruga. Why are you in such a rush to get married? I'm not going anywhere baby," I lied.

"Like I said Khouri, I'm just ready to call you my wife. I don't ever want to lose you baby."

"Marrying me doesn't signify that we'll be together forever either, Ruga. If a quick wedding is what you want then, that's what we'll do. I don't want to lose you either," I lied again.

Truth was, he never had me, but he would know that soon enough. That was as soon as I fucked his world up and paid Paula back.

BOOM!

The door flew open and hit the side of my dresser. It was so hard that it knocked my granite statue of Harriet Tubman down.

"What y'all doing today?" Honestii asked barging up in my bedroom.

"Damn, can't you knock heifer?" I snapped as I got up and straightened up the things on my bureau.

"My bad, what are y'all doing today?" She asked again once she saw Ruga sitting on my bed.

I couldn't believe her ass just completely ignored me like that. She was tripping for real.

"We don't have any plans. What's up?"

"I wanted to know if y'all wanna come out and get a bite to eat with me and bae."

"Naw, I'm not really hungry. We're gonna stay here," I told her assuming Paula was gonna tag her ass right along.

"Come on KK, let's go. We need to get out anyway," Ruga urged me.

"Man, I guess, but where is Paula's ass gon' be at, 'cause she ain't coming and she ain't staying here while we're gone."

"Damn KK, you've been mad hard on Paula lately. What's up with that?"

"Nothing, I'm just tired of sharing everything with her ass," I said cutting my eyes at Ruga.

He didn't say shit. Instead, he sat there like a deer caught in headlights. I wanted to knock his fucking block off. That shit was starting to get to me.

"Honestii please tell your sister to hurry up and marry me. I'm ready to be her husband and she's trippin'."

Just like I thought, Ruga had to be feeling guilty about fucking my cousin. I figured that he was trying to marry me before I found that out.

'Uh, oh, too late nigga!'

"She already said yes nigga. When are you trying to marry her?"

"Shit, we can get married tomorrow," Ruga suggested.

While they talked back and forth my thoughts were interrupted by the money. All I could think about was the come up after I took this nigga for everything.

That was going to be the ultimate lick. Just as soon as I worked out the last little kinks in my plan...

"So, are we going out to eat or what?" I interrupted.

"Damn rudeness yeah let's go down to Felipe's on the west side," Honestii said.

"Like I said before, I'm not hungry, so I don't care where we go eat.

I gathered up my things and soon as everyone was ready, we all piled up in Honestii's ride. They talked the whole way while I stayed deep in thought. I needed to stay focused.

****

After we left the restaurant, we all went back to our house. I made it to the door first, so I used my key and entered in the house with Ruga. My sister and Marlon were trailing close behind.

Once we got into the den, the first thing I saw was Paula. That bitch had the nerve to be flopped on the couch in a bra and fucking boy shorts eating ice cream. I tried to hold in my anger, but I couldn't.

I bum rushed her ass so quick, I almost fell. I had-had enough of that bitch, and she was about to find out just how much.

The second I made it over to the couch, I grabbed the top of her head. Then I started throwing blow after blow until Ruga and Marlon grabbed me up off her ass.

When I was finished with her, she had a black eye, busted lip and a fucked-up nose. I couldn't believe my damn self how badly I had beat her up in such a short time.

"Oh my god Khouri, why did you do that?" Honestii quizzed.

"Look at what this bitch got on! I promised her the last time I caught her like that I would beat that ass!"

"Paula you gotta get yo' shit and get the fuck up out of here," Honestii told her after she saw what she was wearing.

"Where am I supposed to go," she whined.

"I don't give a fuck bitch! Take yo ass to a shelter or something," I barked.

"Baby that is family and family look after family," Ruga butted in.

I must have bit a hole in my lip to stop myself from saying what I really wanted to say. I still flipped the hell out, but I kept that shit somewhat under control.

"Nigga you don't have shit to do with this! Honestii just get her ass before I break something else."

Paula knew what the fuck she was doing. See she was the type of bitch to do something and turn right around and act like she didn't know what she had done. Playing that innocent act and shit! I for one wasn't up for her fuck ass manipulations and mind games.

"Damn Sis," Marlon gasped. "You put hands on ol' girl!"

Ruga was tripping hard when he saw Paula's face. Yes, he knew that I would amp out fast as fuck, but that was the first time he had seen me take shit that far.

"I need a fucking drink!" I huffed as I turned around and headed the opposite direction down the hallway.

Next, I walked into the kitchen to pour me a double shot of Apple Cîroc. I needed to cool down a bit but there came Ruga. He was all up in my fucking space. I prayed he didn't take me there and make me hurt his feelings about fucking my cousin.

He was only a blink away from making me fuck him up too!

"Baby you didn't have to beat ya fam that bad. You know me and Marlon ain't even looking at that girl! She's just doing that shit for attention."

"First of all, don't tell me how I should behave. She was out of line and I corrected that shit! Secondly, she just got all the attention she was asking for," I laughed throwing back my shot. "I guess that bitch learned today!"

Ruga looked at me oddly. He didn't say shit though.

'If he knew what was good for him, he would stay just like that; quiet as a church mouse...'

Honestii

My mind was blown after watching my sister beat Paula's ass, but I could understand why she did it. She had gotten more than enough warnings. I was glad though for real.

Now what did have me boggled was the fact that Paula was eyeing Ruga the whole time she was leaving. Right when she got to the door with her last bag, she set it down and took her cell out.

"I gotta use the bathroom right quick. That is okay ain't it?" Paula smirked as she switched her hips down the hallway. The bitch didn't even wait for a fucking approval.

Feeling curious as to what my cousin was up to, I got up and left Marlon on the couch. First, I made sure Paula did indeed go to the bathroom. Afterwards, I went into the kitchen and checked on my sister to see what was going on with her. I got distracted as soon as I approached the doorway.

"BEEP, BEEP, BEEP-BEEP-BEEP"

Ruga's phone was sitting right on the table where I stopped. I glanced at the screen and read.

Message from Big Booty: I need some ends.

Man, that nigga rushed over to the table and snatched his phone up so damn quick that it made my head spin trying to keep up with his every move. Ruga was being sneaky.

'What the hell is this nigga up to?' I thought as I contemplated on calling his ass out. I quickly changed my mind though once I saw him head to the front.

I just watched as he took his slick ass outside. Khouri was so busy fussing and drinking that she wasn't paying attention to anything going on around her. I was though. I wasn't missing a beat.

"Are you going anywhere tonight?" My sister questioned me with a slur. "I don't know what the hell we're getting into. I just hope that bitch Paula is gone by the time I finish this drink right here!"

Khouri was rambling and delayed me from seeing what her man Ruga was up to. I had to cut her ass off.

"Hold that thought," I blurted out as I held one finger in the air.

Getting up from the stool, I walked to the front room and looked out of the window. All I was able to get a glimpse of was Ruga running back up the stairs.

"Damn, I missed it!" I complained as I turned around to see Marlon standing behind me.

"What did you miss?" He questioned with tight eyes as if he could see right through me.

Before I could answer, Paula came strutting her ass out of the bathroom with a smile as she stared at her screen. That bitch was up to something too. Slowly things were adding up and making much more sense, but the calculations weren't settling with me quite right.

I wasn't about to bring the shit to my sister until I had something solid. All I had right then was a gut feeling and a few observations. That wasn't enough to fuck up my sister wedding; if she was even going through with it. Hell, she was still fucking on Nahmir. She didn't think I knew but I heard them every other morning in the wee hours tearing shit up. I knew it wasn't Ruga because it was always during the time where he opened his business. Khouri wasn't as slick as she thought.

Ignoring all my sister's bullshit, I pulled Marlon by the hand and led him into the kitchen. I wanted to tell my sister that we had finally gotten rid of our cousin Paula. Before I could even get it out, Ruga rushed by me and went directly to Khouri.

"Let's go baby," Ruga suggested as he wrapped his arms around my sister and held her. He glared into her eyes as if she were the most important person on earth.

"Where are we going?" She giggled. Her ass was a little drunk.

"I'm taking you to the lake. Remember we are getting married tomorrow afternoon?" Ruga reminded my sister. "Besides, don't you think we need a little getaway after that shit that just happened?"

"Definitely," Khouri smiled as she stood up. "Let me pack a bag."

They both rushed off and were coming right back after five minutes. Khouri had panties and shit hanging all out of her duffle.

I started to question my sister about her decision to marry Ruga, but I chose not to. It was hers to make and I was not the one to be dishing out any relationship advice; especially when it was unwanted.

"You may wanna pull it together Sis," I teased as she retrieved her keys from the table by the front door.

"Don't worry, I got her Honestii." Ruga assured me as he took the keys from my sister's hand.

"Well, you guys be careful and congratulations," I added sincerely while still having my reservations.

"Thanks," they said in unison before Ruga wrapped his arm around my sister's waist and helped her out of the door.

Soon as it slammed shut behind them, Marlon was all over me. "Damn baby!"

His mouth went from my cheek to my neck to my... Yes, he was taking me there.

I tried to resist him, but his tongue was hitting all the right places. He had me climbing the walls.

"Can we go in the room?" I whispered.

"Why, no one is here?"

I didn't want to have my ass up in the air and someone came waltzing into the house unexpected. Shit, I was still a little traumatized after the last episode of Paula's thot ass invading my private boundaries.

Everything was going through my mind such as my sister coming back after forgetting something or Paula still having a key. Either way, I wasn't taking any chances. I needed my privacy.

"No, I really want to go to my room," I pleaded with my eyes.

Picking me up off my feet, Marlon carried me all the way to my bedroom. That was my comfort zone, but I knew that I soon had to give it up in order to move in with my man and be with him completely. Yes, it was time for me to grow up, but until Marlon set an actual date for our own wedding, I was going to live with my sister.

"Take off all your clothes," he ordered while he turned on Pandora and tuned into 'Donnell Jones Radio'. They were always playing some shit that would get me right up out of my panties.

"Here I go," I laughed silently as I began my show.

As the love making sounds of Tyrese blared through the wireless speakers, I twirled my hips and did a little striptease to get shit started. Marlon could barely contain himself.

"You like?" I whispered as I straddled him in the chair then grinded up against his hardness.

I was making myself extremely wet and was becoming turned on more by the second, especially when I reversed it and reached down to grab my ankles.

Marlon gripped my hips and met every thrust I threw back at him. I knew if we didn't stop that he would soon be busting a good old nut right there in his pants.

"No, no, wait, wait!" He pleaded as he eased me up and came out of his clothes. "Fuck that, I need to feel all of you baby…"

I removed my panties and met Marlon on the bed. That was where he gently eased me on my back and spread my legs.

Taking his time, he kissed me starting at my ankles. When he got to my thighs, I couldn't take the teasing. Fuck the foreplay. I needed the dick.

"Give it to me baby," I begged in a whisper.

"Let me taste you first."

"Noooooo baby…I want you. I need you!" I continued looking at him with pure lust. I was craving him.

"I got you, baby," Marlon assured as he hovered over me before entering me and penetrating me at a slow pace.

I wrapped my legs around him and squeezed hard so that I could control the momentum. I wanted it faster and harder. I needed to cum.

"Yes, shit yes!" I shouted as I released my first orgasm.

My nails dug deeply into the smooth chocolate skin on Marlon's back. I knew I had to have drawn blood, but I couldn't help myself.

"Shit baby!" he yelled out as he clinched my body so tight that it prevented me from trying to get another sexual explosion. Shit, I was horny...

Marlon let go of me several moments later only to roll over and expose his flat tire. So much for me getting some more dick right then...

Khouri

I sure as hell had my sister fooled thinking that I was drunk and unaware of Ruga's actions, but I had to play the role. I needed to get him right where I wanted him and if going to the lake was part of it then so be it.

"Baby, why did you jump on ya cousin like that," Ruga asked again as soon as we hopped on the highway.

"I'd rather not talk about that right now baby. Let's just relax and enjoy one another's company," I replied as I reclined my seat and slid my sunglasses over my eyes.

To be honest, the ride was just beginning to relax me. Then, he just had to go and mention Paula's name and ruin my fucking moment.

Closing my eyes, I allowed my mind to wander off. No matter how hard I tried to focus, my mind kept going to Nahmir. He was very upset with me and I knew it was because he loved me, well I hoped he did. He never wanted to tell me, but I knew he did.

'RING, BEEP, RING, BEEP,'

"Is that your cell?" Ruga asked while turning down the music.

"Yeah, it's probably just my sister trying to check on me. I'll call her back in a few." I lied. I knew exactly who it was by the ringtone. It was Nahmir.

Things got awkwardly silent. It had to be at least two minutes that passed before Ruga spoke again.

"Are you hungry?"

"No, but I'm thirsty as hell."

"Aight, I'm about to hop off at the next exit and get me a burger or something. A nigga starving over here," Ruga laughed as he veered into the right lane.

When we got off the highway, there was a little country diner. I wasn't feeling it at all, so I just had Ruga bring me some fries and a soda out.

Watching Ruga as he entered the older worn out structure that looked like it was barely standing, I decided on calling Nahmir. I knew that it was him blowing up my cell. The only reason he was doing that was because he was worried about me fucking with Ruga.

Sure, that was what I was doing but Nahmir was going to have to bear with me. It was something that I had to do in order to take my sister's advice and get out of the game altogether while I could.

I needed to call him. Reaching into my handbag, I drew out my cell to dial his number. Before I could complete the action, my phone sang out.

'RING, RING'

It was Nahmir. I answered it right away.

"Hey baby," he chanted like he was in a good mood.

"Hey boo, I was just about to call you."

"Is that right?"

"Sho' nuff," I giggled.

"Well tell me baby, what's up?"

I began telling him about my time with Ruga. I explained my plan thoroughly and he was quiet until I got to the part about marrying him.

"So, your telling me that you gotta marry that nigga to get that bag?" He huffed. "Sounds to me like some bullshit Khouri."

"It ain't," I assured him as I filled him in on the hundreds of thousands Ruga was worth.

"I don't care if the nigga is a millionaire. I ain't feelin' you are being with him like that Khouri

Tell me this...You fuckin' that nigga?"

"No!" I snapped.

"Have you been intimate with that nigga?" he probed backing me in a corner to tell him a lie.

"No! I told him we had to wait until we got married..."

"Oh, so you gonna fuck him then?"

"No..."

"That's what the fuck you just said yo!" he barked.

I hurried to calm him down once I promised that I wasn't thinking about another man. Trust me, I laid that shit on so thick I impressed my damn self.

Once we hung up, I knew deep down that Nahmir was bothered by the whole arrangement and didn't trust it. He had no reason not to though. As far as Ruga went, I had absolutely no love for him...

The way my life had been going, my little plan was liable to blow up in my face. My greatest fear at that point was messing up the lick with Ruga, losing Nahmir all together and worse than that, losing my damn life.

Instead of worrying about it right then, I grabbed the bottle out of the backseat. I wanted to stay drunk the entire time so that I wouldn't worry about Nahmir. I couldn't allow that to cloud my judgment. I had to stay focused in order to complete my mission.

"Damn, here this nigga come..." I huffed as I shoved the bottle of alcohol back into the pouch on the back of my seat.

"Here you go baby," Ruga smiled as he climbed into the car and handed me a bag. When he released it, he kissed me on my cheek.

Ugh!

I didn't even want him to touch me. My promise to Nahmir was about to keep.

Hopefully it won't be too hard. I thought to myself as we finally arrived at the lake.

We went inside and set our bags down. Suddenly I came up with the perfect notion.

Running into the bathroom after grabbing my side, I faked like I got my period. I knew that was the one thing that would keep Ruga off me. That idea was right on time…

That was the perfect excuse not to sleep with Ruga yet. I knew that bought me at least and extra five days.

Lucky me…

****

The next morning when Ruga and I got up, we showered, dressed and headed home. We had to hurry and get there in order to be on time for the informal ceremony we had planned later that day at the courthouse.

The second we got in the car to leave, I popped a mild muscle relaxer and slept all the way home. The drowsiness was so overwhelming that it was difficult to climb out of the car and make it inside. Ruga had to help me.

Now when I walked in, Honestii and Marlon made sure they woke me all the way up with their crazy jokes. They just had to start with the teasing shit, and I wasn't up for it.

"Here comes the bride," my sister sang out as I came in the door.

"All dressed in white," Marlon followed in song.

"Oh, y'all muthafuckas are real funny right? Yup, today is my wedding day niggas," I replied jokingly.

Honestii had drinks and finger foods all laid out for us, so y'all know my ass was all up in that.

"I still can't believe ya old ass is getting married today. Have you heard from Nahmir?" Honestii whispered.

"Yeah, I can't believe it either and no I haven't spoken to him since yesterday," I replied quietly.

"Did you tell him about marrying Ruga?"

"Yeah girl," I sighed.

"I take it that it didn't go too well huh?"

"No, but I'll figure that all out later," I told my sister in an annoyed tone.

"Well, what about the honeymoon? Are y'all gonna have one?" Honestii pried changing the subject.

"Not yet, I haven't decided when we should have one," I responded and began to tell her some shit. "Look there are some things that you don't know just yet sissy, but shit is about to get really messy. Don't worry, I'll tell you about everything real soon because I can barely hold it in."

"I know you better tell me now sis," Honestii insisted.

"Hush that up, I'm gonna tell you very soon. just chill," I said trying to reassure her.

We threw a few drinks back and then Ruga and I headed upstairs to get ready for the day.

"Baby, I'm nervous," Ruga admitted.

"Why, you love me, and I love you and that's all that matters. We're in this 'til the end Lenard," I lied to him using his government name. He needed to know that I was very serious.

"I'm afraid that I won't be good enough for you or something," he frowned.

"You just have cold feet baby, don't sweat it, we're gonna be alright."

I walked over to where he was standing and kissed his lips. I had to convince him that the words I had just spoken were sincere.

I think I was more nervous than he was to be honest, but I knew what had to be done. There was no backing down now. I had to get some payback. This pussy hoe ass nigga couldn't possibly think it was okay for his ass to fuck on my cousin and there wouldn't be repercussions...

"Let's get ready," Ruga suggested as he led me to the bathroom.

We showered and dressed in our all-white linen outfits. His was a pantsuit and mine was a full-length strapless dress with the back out.

I had chosen not to wear a veil because it was too cliché. Besides that, we were getting married at the fucking Justice of the Peace. There was no reason to go all out for that place. Especially when this shit was fake in my eyes. I just needed some basic shit.

****

A couple of hours later when we arrived downtown, there was a short wait. The entire time Honestii chatted about a little bit of everything. I couldn't even shut her ass up if I tried and trust me, I tried.

With all that talking I could barely focus on my thoughts. My mind was everywhere but on the matter at hand.

Marlon and Ruga were talking the whole wait time, didn't help either. They wouldn't hush it up when I gave them the evil eye. They just kept right on yapping.

After another half hour or so, it was finally our turn to see the judge. Ruga held my sweaty ass hand all the way over to the altar positioned in the corner of a small room. The ordained judge recited the vows. We didn't have to repeat but two words.

I swallowed several lumps in my throat before I tried my best to spit them out.

"I do..."

We were then pronounced husband and wife. Reality kicked in causing my heart to drop.

'I must be fuckin' crazy!'

I turned to look at the huge smile that Ruga wore. It appeared as if he had just hit the lottery when in all reality, I was the one who was about to secretly hit it...

After the nervousness settled, we finally kissed. Little did that nigga know, that was his *'goodbye kiss'*. My plan was about to be in full effect as soon as possible.

"KK!" Honestii called out. "We need to sign these last papers."

Holding hands, Ruga and I eased on over to my sister and Marlon. They were positioned at the other end of the altar.

The clergyman was waiting right there for us with all the proper documentation we had to go over. It was quick and when we dotted the last 'I' we were on our way out of there.

Fucked up thing was, when we left the Courthouse, I had an alert that our silent alarm had gone off. That meant someone was at our place without an invitation.

We couldn't get home quick enough...

Honestii

When the security company alerted both me and my sister that there was an intruder in our home, they assured us that the police were on their way. It didn't matter to us because we still rushed there to see what damage was done.

All I could think about was all the money we had stashed there. It was most of our life savings seeing that neither of us had over ten thousand in the bank each. We didn't trust them, but I wish we had of...

"You think that someone could have lifted our safe's?" Khouri whispered as we flew up the road that led to our place.

"I sure in hell hope not man," I replied nervously as we arrived.

The police were already there but they hadn't gone in yet. Everyone unbuckled and hopped out quickly and rushed the officers before they could do so.

"Are you the owner of this property?" the short stubby cop questioned with his hand on his government issued weapon.

"Yes sir," Khouri interjected and pulled out her identification.

The cop took it from her and held it in the air to check the address. Next he escorted her to the door to key in the code to the alarm.

"I'm going to come inside with you and check to make sure no one is in there and then you can see if anything is missing."

I nodded as Khouri and I entered the house behind him and two of his partners. They drew their guns and went from room to room while we stayed in the foyer. I didn't have a problem with that. I wasn't trying to get shot or some shit.

"What about the guns?" I whispered remembering that I had them in a case in the back of my closet. I just prayed that they were either stolen or the police officers would overlook them.

"Clear, clear, clear," they each yelled out.

"Someone made a pretty good mess. It looks like they were searching for something specific, but they're gone now. Are you ready to go check things out?" The tall brown skinned cop questioned as he escorted us to the living room where there were broken items everywhere. "You know who would want something from you?"

"Ah, that would be a no! We don't sell drugs and we don't have enough money for anyone to break in to get!" Khouri barked as the officer eyed Ruga from head to toe.

I could see why though. That nigga was still dressed like he was in the streets even though he had enough paper to wear a designer suit everyday if he chose to.

Dragging Khouri to the back, we went to check everything. She was the one that yelled my name first but before I could go to her, I had to make sure my stash in the bathroom cabinet was secure. That was where most of my cash was. I only kept about five bands in my decoy safe, which I saw was gone as soon as I stepped inside my closet.

"Shit!"

I put my face in my hands and took a deep breath to stop from crying. Some of my mother's jewelry was in there. They weren't valuable pieces, but the sentimental value was irreplaceable.

Ugh! I grunted instead of screaming. Afterwards, I closed my eyes and regulated my breathing. I had to pull it together before going back in there with the police.

Immediately remembering about the stash of weapons we had, I went to the back of my closet and drew the blankets up. To my surprise there sat the case with all guns accounted for. That was a relief.

"Honestii!" my sister yelled out once again. It sounded like she was even more irritated than before.

I covered the cases back up while taking a mental note to get rid of all of them as soon as possible. When I finished, I went to see what my sister was hollering about.

"What is it?"

"Look at this shit right here," Khouri whispered as she held up one of Paula's sterling silver butterfly earrings with a single diamond. "It had to be that bitch! It was right here, where my safe was that had my money and jewelry in it!"

"All ya money?" I whispered grabbing my mouth.

"Hell, no sis," Khouri grinned sneakily as she drew a large metal box from beneath her bed. "The bitch didn't find my real stash, but she did get some of my nice jewelry."

"Yeah Sis, mine too, and momma's stuff," I confessed sadly. My sister hurried over to me to console me.

Suddenly I came up with a bright idea. I pulled away from Khouri and let her in on it.

"Sis let's just do a simple report on the jewelry. I want to take care of this shit with Paula myself. That bitch is about to pay for this!"

"I gotta better one sis! Remember I told you about that plan?"

"Yeah," I answered easing a little closer so that I could hear Khouri whispering.

"Well the shit is right on time. I can't tell you the whole thing right now but just know that I have a little something lined up. We are about to use Paula to take the fall! We're about to set that bitch up!"

I wanted to ask my sister a dozen questions, but I knew that it wasn't the time. We still had Ruga and Marlon waiting on us, right along with quite a few cops in the living room.

"Come on KK," I urged. "Let's go back in there and handle this and then we can discuss all this when we get a few minutes alone."

We agreed and then went to find a cop to take our statement. I was about to claim every piece I had in my safe; even the stolen ones. My homeowners would back me up because my slick ass documented all my shit that I purchased and had receipts for. The police would send a 'stolen item' report to all the pawn shops in the state so if Paula tried to hawk my shit for cash she would be arrested on sight. I hoped silently that she was that stupid.

If not, I was still going to pay Paula back. That was almost fifteen bands plus the jewelry she took from the both of us together. For us, it wasn't the amount. It was the principle.

"Damn, who you think did some shit like this?" Ruga questioned as he followed Honestii to the back.

"I have no idea..." Khouri sang before closing them in her bedroom.

I sighed and turned around only to find Marlon cleaning up. He was hanging pictures back up and picking up the broken pieces of my favorite lamp. It used to be my mother's.

Tears came to my eyes as I bent down to help my man. Soon as he saw me crying, he stopped. "What's wrong? Do you know who did this?"

"No," I lied without facing him.

"Be honest with me right now baby," Marlon begged and forced eye contact. "Have you and your sister still been lickin' niggas? Is that who could have come up in here and did this shit? Now what would've happened if you were home alone and they came up in here? What then Honestii?"

The tone of his voice sent chills down my whole body. He was seriously heated for the wrong reason.

I wanted so desperately to tell him that Paula was behind this shit, but I had already promised my sister that I wouldn't. That gave me no choice but to continue to lie.

"No, we haven't been doing any of that bae!" I answered. "So, it couldn't be behind that."

"Well I don't like the shit and I have a real bad feeling about it."

"About what babe?"

"About you guys getting robbed and the only thing they take is jewelry. What about all these high-tech gadgets you guys have. All of them are brand new and easy to carry out. Tell me why they didn't take anything else?"

"How the hell am I supposed to know baby?" I snapped. "I don't even know who did the shit!"

Marlon looked at me as if he could see through my lies, but I stuck with them. He couldn't break me when it came to keep my word to my sister...

"Come on, I know your room is a mess huh?" he questioned as he took me by the hand

and led me to my bedroom. "We might as well clean that shit up too."

Soon as we got to the room, we began putting everything back in place. That shit lasted all of five minutes before I slid everything that was on my bed, onto the floor. I needed some room to get me some. I needed a stress reliever.

"Oh, so you want some huh?" Marlon teased as he neared me and began to undress me. "I think I can help you out with that request."

Pulling my naked body against his, Marlon wrapped me up in his arms and pressed his lips against the left side of my neck.

By the sounds of his moans and the stiffness of his dick, I knew that my man was ready to give my body all the attention it was craving.

That day I wanted to be touched in a way that would make me lose touch with reality, if only for a few moments. I would take it.

When we were done, I went to the bathroom to clean myself up. I locked myself in and reached in the cabinet behind the mirror to get my toothbrush. That was when I saw my birth control pills.

"Damn," I gasped as I slid them out and opened the case. "When was the last time I took one of these?"

Taking a deep breath, I counted the days. There were too many and it was too late.

"Oh, my goodness," I huffed becoming anxious. I couldn't believe I had been that careless.

As I stood there speechless, I prayed that I hadn't gotten myself knocked up. I wasn't ready for that...

Khouri

After Ruga hounded me all night to move in with him, I had no choice to at least go over there, but as soon as his ass was snoring, I rushed over to Nahmir's place with tear filled eyes. I told him everything that had transpired. I came clean about everything. I had no choice once Ruga started pressuring me to be with him fully. That just wasn't going to happen, husband or not. Besides, Nahmir wasn't going for it. Of course, I didn't have to tell him if I had decided to go all the way, but I didn't want to lie anymore.

With me telling him about Ruga, he decided to come clean about his feelings for me. It was only for that moment then he got straight to business.

"Look, fuck scamming on that nigga. I got a better one."

Nahmir ran down just how we were going to hit our mark. It was going to be a lovely payout, but it still didn't change my mind about paying Ruga and Paula back. I was just going to keep that to myself for the time being. There was no need to shake the bush when everything was cool for the moment.

"So, you down?" He quizzed looking me in the eye. "This nigga Spider got hella bread baby?

"Word? It's like that," I smirked.

"Fuck Yeah! Just forget about the shit with Ruga. You got that? I want you divorced from that nigga by the end of the week," he huffed as he released me and stood up to start pacing. "I swear to you if I knew that y'all was at the fuckin' courthouse today I would have been there to blow all that lil' shit out of the water..."

"Why, why Slim?" I blurted out. "Is it because you love me?"

"You know I care about you. You my shorty and I don't like to be played with. I don't give a fuck about a lick! I care about loyalty."

"So, you want me to be loyal while you're out here fucking any bitch you want?"

"I ain't been up in anybody but you since our last altercation behind Bella! That's on my fuckin' mama yo!" He yelled out becoming more upset. "I'm out here trying to get shit set up for us... You know what? Fuck it! Let's just get to business. Are you sure that you and your sister are ready to play with the big dogs?"

"Nigga, I done told you. I'm ready for whatever when it comes to getting this bag. I just want it to be my final run at this shit. I want out after this shit!"

"My word baby, we're both out after this shit," He spoke calmly as he graced my lips with his. It was a small peck that quickly grew into a passionate kiss. Before I knew it, my panties were moist.

When Nahmir let me loose, he stared in my eyes. I just knew he was about to say those three words I had been dying to hear but instead he began talking about business again.

'Ugh! I just wanted to hear it one time.'

"Alright, if you think you're ready then let's do this. The only thing is that I will be driving you and Honestii over there, so I can have your back in case some shit pop off, 'cause this nigga is real reckless baby," he said rubbing my thighs.

"Okay baby," I giggled while he tried to give me some last details about the hit. All the while he was undressing me.

I knew exactly what he was doing. He wanted some of my goodies, and I was more than happy to oblige...

****

It wasn't until the next morning when I got back home. Ruga was up with a very big attitude because he couldn't get in touch with me. Now you know I didn't give a fuck!

"Baby I needed to take some time to myself and clear my head," I lied.

"Fuck that Khouri, you could have left me a message or at least answered ya phone when I was calling you like ten times!"

"First of all, don't ever talk to me like that nigga! I'm your wife, not your property! If I said I needed some time to myself then that's all it was! I left my phone in the car while I sat out by the lake for a while."

"Baby all I'm saying is that we haven't even been married a good week and you're already playing disappearing acts and shit. You gotta let me know where you are. I be worried and shit!"

"Ruga, you are my husband, not my damn daddy. I married you because I love you, but you need to know that you can't control me, like I said, I needed some time to myself, damn!"

I knew that Ruga was starting to suspect something when I had stayed out all night, but I didn't think that he would be on my ass like that. In the future I would have to be more careful.

I quickly walked in the kitchen and put my little ass burner cell in the junk drawer. I powered it off before I did so that Nahmir wouldn't call while Ruga was in there. Unfortunately, that was the only way for us to communicate.

"What the fuck is going on with you Khouri? You know ever since we been married, you been on some other shit."

"I'm the same person as before, and what do you mean, since we been married. We been married for a few days. That's hardly enough time to say I'm trippin'."

I wanted to spaz on his ass. The only reason why I didn't go there was because he was looking like a helpless little puppy. I just left it alone.

"Look baby, I'm sorry for upsetting you. I was just worried about you. I don't ever want to lose you," Ruga blurted out like he was getting a little emotional and shit.

I bet he wasn't feeling like that when he was power driving his dick in my cousin's funky ass pussy though!

I sucked my ill thought up first. Then I responded.

"No don't apologize Ruga, I was being a brat. I'm the one that's sorry for acting like I was. I love you baby, and nothing like this will happen again. You have my word." I said crossing my fingers behind my back like a little ass kid.

I had to smooth things over with his ass if my plans were going to work out without a flaw. There was no way that I was about to fuck that up.

"I'm about to change and go to my house…"

"Are we going to get your stuff?"

"Here you go," I complained as I got my clothes to go and shower. "I don't feel like moving a damn thing."

He didn't push it. He just made sure that he was ready to go when I got out of the bathroom. He even stayed quiet the entire ride over there.

"Hey y'all," Honestii and Marlon greeted us in unison.

They were already up and dressed. I waved, smiled and went into the kitchen. Ruga was right behind me. He sure didn't have shit to say in the car but as soon as we got to my house the nigga started whining about everything. He didn't shut the hell up until his cell phone rang with Paula's number. That shit had me heated and I called him on it quick.

Before Ruga had time to give me some lame ass excuse, my sister was joining us. That was his cue to shut up.

"Are y'all good now?" Honestii asked walking in right behind me with a wide grin.

"Yeah, we're straight," I told her kissing Ruga on the lips. "Baby, can you go in there with Marlon while I chop it up with my sister really quick?"

"No doubt baby just don't talk too much shit about me," Ruga replied jokingly as he left the room.

"What's up sis, why did we need to be alone?" Honestii quizzed. "I hope it's to finally tell me about what the hell got you so mad at Paula again. Is she calling Ruga?"

"Yes, sis and I have something to tell you, but I need for you to chill."

"Don't tell me to chill KK, what's going on?" She pressed.

"Please don't get mad at me, but remember that night about a month ago when I came home asking where Paula's ass was?"

"Yeah, and?"

"Well, I had just caught her ass over Ruga's crib bent over."

"What the fuck are you telling me bitch?" She snapped with a raised brow.

"I'm telling you that Ruga and Paula was fuckin' but don't sweat it because I have something in store for both of their ass," I whispered pouring me a drink of vodka.

"So why the fuck did you marry that fuckboy ass nigga then?"

"I simply married him because his ass will be the ultimate lick. He has plenty of money and that big ol' house, silly ass nigga. Don't forget that I get half of everything."

At first, I didn't want to tell my sister, but this shit was about to come to light and she needed to know what to expect.

"So, this whole marriage thing is fake?" Honestii whispered before covering her mouth.

"Hell yeah, I don't love that pussy hole!"

"So, you did it just so you could lick him KK?" Honestii checked.

"Yes girl! Fuckin' on a scamming ass rich ass nigga," I replied laughing at myself.

"Oh, fuck yeah KK, your ass is a fuckin' evil genius!" My sister gasped. "I thought you were done?"

"Never underestimate me, I'm always on my shit even when it seems like I'm not," she replied.

"So besides paying Ruga's cheating ass back, what are we gonna do about Paula?"

"I don't know yet, but we'll think of something," I told her then brought up the shit Nahmir had set up.

"So, let's just focus on this lick and worry about Ruga and Paula afterwards," my sister suggested.

"Yeah, I'm gonna put that shit on the backburner until Ruga stops being so suspicious. But it gotta be soon because I ain't trying to fuck that nigga. Only one going up in this good stuff is Nahmir," I clowned in a hushed tone. "I just need you to help me with this last lick."

"Oh, I got you sissy. Don't you worry about shit, I always gotcha back," Honestii told me.

"We got this just watch how I work," I told her with only the intentions of taking care of business then getting out the game. Nahmir and I were going to get our happily ever after if I had to die trying to get it for us...

Honestii

When my sister revealed the secret that she had been keeping, she nearly blew my mind. I couldn't believe how she caught Ruga and Paula fucking! I had a good feeling that they were creeping around. I just couldn't prove it! That was a scandalous hoe for real!

She not only stole our money, the bitch fucked Khouri's man! We had to get her ass back... good and I knew just the thing. I had to wait until I had a free moment to start setting it up.

"Come on, let's go out here with the guys before they come up in here being nosey," Khouri suggested as she got up and headed out of the kitchen. I was right behind her.

"What's up baby?" Marlon questioned when my sister and I walked into the family room where he and Ruga were watching the Dallas Cowboys whoop on the Detroit Lions in the second to the last game before the playoffs started. They were hollering like it was the Super Bowl.

"Get em' Cowboys!" Marlon shouted.

"Fuck that! Yes! You see that interception?" Ruga yelled back.

While they were all wrapped in their game, I snuck off to call Paula to put my plan in full effect. I had a proposition for her ass. I was about to let her hit the lick with us; only I was going to set her ass up. I wasn't going to run it by my sister or Nahmir until I knew for sure Paula was with it.

I found my cell in my room and quickly dialed my cousin's number. She picked up right away.

"What?" Paula answered rudely. I ignored her stupid ass and continued with my spill.

"Hey girl, you know we got robbed yesterday?" I huffed as I turned up my nose and closed my bedroom door to obtain a bit of privacy.

Meanwhile, that bitch Paula must have gotten tongue tied because it took her a few seconds to spit some shit out. When she did, I could tell that she was lying.

"Say what? I wonder who would do some bold ass shit like that? They just came up in there and only took your money?" She replied.

"Yeah, but now we have this lick set up and we can get all that shit back plus an extra half mil a piece. You down?" I asked trying to be convincing. "We know the dudes that stole the shit."

"Y'all do?" She sang like she was shocked.

'Ol' dramatic ass bitch.'

"Yeah, you wanna get down?" I repeated knowing that the little bit of ends she got from us wasn't shit and wouldn't last her long. That was if she could even get into our safe's without help. Although they were small, they both needed keys and had combination locks as well.

"Seriously, you would let me get down with you guys?" Paula checked sounding extremely anxious.

"Hell yeah, you family girl! Fuck all that other shit! You are the only one that we can trust. Plus, we need someone to run interference while we get, they ass! You don't have to do nothing else and we'll still give you a fair cut! We really need you cousin."

"Hell yeah, but is your sister cool with it?" Paula questioned hesitantly. "Cause I don't need no trouble. I'm trying to get my life right."

"That's why I called you. It was Khouri's idea!" I lied. "This lick right here will make sure you're straight for a long time. Trust me cousin! You want this bag we about to come up on. I need the shit and I damn sho' know you do,"

Just like a greedy bitch would do... She took the bait with ease! Paula was just the fucking snake I knew her to be, but she was about to get a dose of her own venom.

"Okay check this shit out," I said giving Paula the made-up details about the robbery. "Just be ready when I call you and make sure you wear some of that shit you be wearing at the house. You know that shit that be having ya tits and ass hanging out?"

"Yeah."

"Aight, you'll hear from me real soon."

"Bet!"

When I hung up and turned around, I bumped right into Khouri's ass. "It was my idea huh?"

"Well, ah, you see..."

"No, what the hell I see is you having one hell of a plan to bring her into this shit and it better include her biting the dust."

I told my sister how I factored Paula into the plan. Once she heard what I had in mind she was all for it. That sneaky look in her eye told me so.

"What the hell are you two talking about?" Marlon questioned before Khouri had the opportunity to respond. "Never mind, I don't even wanna know."

"What's up baby," I asked him while giving him a hug.

"I just got a call from the office and I gotta go take care of some things out of town. I'll be gone for a couple of days or so. You gonna be aight without me?"

"Yeah her ass is gonna be just fine. I got plenty of shit for her to do here," my sister spoke as she butted in.

"Yeah, I bet," he smirked.

"When are you leaving baby?" I asked after giving my sister the *'stank face'*.

"I gotta go right now so I can pack and make it to the airport. You feel like taking me baby?"

I agreed only to hurry him off. I needed him out of the way while we hit the lick. He was the last person that I needed badgering me and shit.

I took him to his house, helped him throw some shit in a suitcase, fucked the shit out of him then dropped his ass off at the airport.

Mission accomplished...

"What does she want now?" I huffed looking down at my cell only to see Paula's name come up. I tried my best to keep my eyes trained to the highway while I answered it.

"What's up?" I asked curiously.

"I was just thinking about what you said about y'all getting robbed. I don't have much but if y'all need anything let me know," she spoke trying her damnedest to sound sincere. I wasn't falling for the shit though; not one bit. She had me fucked up if she even thought that I did!

"No, that's so sweet Paula," I replied trying to refrain from giving her a piece of my mind. You see she wasn't the only one that had acting skills. "Marlon took care of everything."

"What, that nigga Ruga didn't kick in? Didn't he just marry Khouri?" She questioned a little too nosily for me.

"That nigga is being tight with his money for some reason. I thought that shit was shady too but I'm gonna mind my own business and handle this shit! You still down?"

"You already know cousin," Paula boasted like the bad bitch she wasn't. "I stay ready!"

"Blah, blah, blah," I thought feeling irritated as I got off on my exit.

I had to hurry up and hang up the phone with her dumb ass. She was truly something special and I didn't mean in a good way either...

"Home sweet home," I chanted as I turned on my block. Right away I noticed that Ruga's car was gone, and its place sat Nahmir's brand new royal blue G-Wagon. That shit was nice.

"What the fuck is going on in here?" I asked looking at my sister who was in next to nothing. All her skin was showing, displaying all her many tattoo's. She was obsessed with that shit.

Khouri quickly got dressed in all black and then had the nerve to throw on a short blond wig. "Oh, I forgot something," she mumbled as she stepped into the closet and came out holding the biggest gun I had ever seen in my life.

"Where the hell did you get that?" I gasped.

"She ain't using this shit," Nahmir laughed as he entered the room and snatched the weapon out of my sister's hand. He then placed it by the sofa. "She can barely handle a damn .40 cal. You think I'm gonna let her fuck with that?"

"Whatever Slim," Khouri fussed. "You always talkin' shit."

"You love me though," he flirted.

"You love me?" She asked immediately.

"Girl hush and get ready," he smirked and left the room.

I was so fucking lost. My sister was married to a nigga that she caught fucking her cousin but all the while she was still sleeping with and in love with Nahmir.

Boy, I'll tell you...

Khouri

It was time to hit the lick and I couldn't get rid of Ruga to save my fucking life. He was supposed to be gone to pick up some cars earlier that day, but that nigga had been lounging around his house for hours. I had to think of something else.

"I'm thirsty baby, can you get me some juice or something?" Ruga asked.

"I gotcha," I chanted.

Making a hasty decision on my way to the kitchen, I stopped by the bathroom to grab a few pain reliever p.m. capsules. I took them, opened about four or five up and dumped the contents into a small glass of fruit punch then added some ice. I knew if it were only a little juice, he would drink it all at once with his thirsty ass.

Using my finger, I stirred it around. Then I went back to the bedroom to give it to him.

"Thanks baby," he smiled as he downed the whole glass and held out the empty tumbler. "Can you get me a little more please? I don't know why you got me that lil' ass glass."

Ignoring his smart-ass remark, I snatched up his tumbler, refilled it then took it back to him. He downed it once again but this time he set the glass down on the table beside the bed and continued watching television.

I left his ass right there while I went outside to my car. I had to get to my burner cell to dial Nahmir back.

"What the fuck are you doing yo?" Nahmir barked. "I know you at that nigga's house! I told you to end that shit Khouri!"

"Are you seriously arguing with me right now? I have to get his cell for the set up remember?"

"Yeah, now bring yo' ass on!" He shouted aggressively. "It shouldn't take you that fuckin' long to get a damn phone!"

"Look, let me do this! Now I'm leaving here in the next half hour. Meet me at your spot. I'll call my sister and have her tell Paula."

"Be there Khouri! Don't have me come for you," he threatened. "If you ain't here in thirty, I'm coming over to that niggas house. You think I don't know where that nigga stays at?"

"Shut that shit up! I'll be there, Nahmir, bye!"

I hung up the phone and placed it under the seat before returning in the house. I immediately ran up the stairs to go check on Ruga.

"Look at this shit right here." I laughed as I watched my so called *'husband'* snore loudly. He was out like a light.

I hurried up and snatched his cell and put in my pocket. I would need that shit later to plant at Spider's spot.

As I drove to Nahmir's house, my mind stayed on Paula. I knew what Ruga's fate would be, but I was still debating on whether not to go with Honestii's plan to get our cousin caught up too.

I really didn't want her dead, even though she stole all our money. But, if I did let her live, she would be sure to tell on us.

There I was, caught in a dilemma and I was already arriving at Nahmir's. I had decisions to make.

What the fuck am I gonna do? I might just have to roll with my sister's plan...

I got out the car feeling a little nervous, but I was able to shake it off and enter the house confidently. *Never let them see you sweat...*

"Y'all ready for this shit?" Nahmir spoke as he handed me my gear.

My sister and Paula were standing there looking all focused and shit. I paid them no mind and began putting my black sneakers on. I pulled my hood up over my blonde wig and waited for everyone else to get ready.

"We are gonna all ride together. Honestii up front with me and Khouri you ride in the back with Paula," he instructed.

I didn't know what the fuck he was on. That was not what the hell we discussed.

"What?"

"Khouri, let me do this okay baby?"

I smirked at him and then headed outside first. I paced back and forth as I lit a cigarette. I rarely smoked but when I was super stressed, I had to. Shit, I hated last minute changes.

"Fuck it," I thought. I had to get my money with a side of revenge. That was all I wanted. A lover's quarrel could wait.

"Come on KK," Honestii motioned as she came out behind me and walked to the car. "We got this Sis."

"We need to leave here now and go straight to Spider's. We need to time it just right," Nahmir barked as he popped the locks and hopped in the driver's seat.

I waved that nigga off and got in the back with Honestii. That left Paula to sit in the front. Slim immediately mean mugged me as she slid her trashy ass in.

Nahmir turned around without a word and pulled off. He wasted no time to end the silence by turning on the radio to the hip-hop station. That gave me the chance to talk to my sister.

"You send Paula up to the door and have her act like her dumb ass is lost. You know them thirsty nigga's gonna let her in."

"Hell yeah," Honestii agreed. "I don't know what she's up to but before you got to the Nahmir's house, I caught Paula on the phone whispering on her cell. I'll make sure to take that shit from her soon as we get out."

"Cool, but be careful Sis," I warned. I didn't trust Paula one fucking bit.

"Let's just go in here and get this money."

"Cool, I'm down."

Honestii got her deuce-deuce and nine and tucked them away before pulling her forty-five out.

"Hit the lights!" I instructed as Nahmir pulled down the dark road and parked.

"I'm gonna send...," he began.

"I got this," Paula interrupted as she reached for the door handle.

Nahmir hit the locks securing us inside. "Y'all know what to do?"

"Yes, but I need you to give me your cell first," Honestii insisted.

"For what?"

"Because I don't need that shit going off! Now give it to her!" Nahmir barked so harshly that it caused me to tremble.

Paula hurried to dig her phone out of her purse. Then she tossed it into the backseat between me and my sister.

"There, y'all trippin'," she smirked. "Can I get out now?"

"You know what you're doing because..."

"I said I got this!" Paula snapped as she quickly unlocked her own door and got out.

Before hurrying off, she displayed a small handgun she had. It was the same one I clipped from Ruga that first night I went over his house. It had to be it. I could tell by the gold trim and the initials.

"Wait!" I yelled.

"Nah, let that bitch go. If she gets fucked up that's on her. I'm still going up in there to get the money. We'll be long gone before them lil' niggas can even think about calling for backup."

"Okay since Paula wanna be the decoy, you two go around back and I'll come through the front," Nahmir instructed. "But don't come in until you hear me yell 'One'."

Seconds after Nahmir finished telling us what to do there was a gunshot. My vision went straight to Spider's door. It was Paula. She shot some tall dude causing his body to drop at her feet.

'POP, POP'

Two more shots followed. That was when Paula's body came crashing down on top of the guy she had just killed.

'POP, POP'

There went Nahmir, straight to the door, shooting and killing two men wearing hoodies. Khouri and I hurried out and ran around to the back.

"I can't believe that nigga killed Paula!" Honestii huffed like she was pumping herself up to get madder. "Are we walking into a fucking trap?"

Hushing her up, I held my hand to her mouth and led her through the back door.

"Maybe we should just go," my sister mumbled as she held on to my arm.

"No, we need this, and plus we gotta make sure to tie up any loose ends!" I reminded my sister.

"One!" We heard Nahmir yell out.

My sister toughened up quick and got in front of me and led the way through the unlocked rear door that led into a laundry room. When she opened the second door, there was silence.

As we started down the hallway, I saw the reflection of a guy with a gun in the mirror that was hanging on the wall. Without thinking, I lunged my body in front of my sisters to shield her from the hot bullets that flew toward us. We both hit the floor and began firing.

When the smoke settled a bit, there was Nahmir. He was holding three big bags.

"Come on y'all!" He snapped.

'POP, POP'

A short stubby guy came out of nowhere and began shooting towards us. Honestii was able to move but I was wounded.

"Get the fuck down!" Nahmir shouted as he shoved Honestii and threw himself on top of me.

'POP, POP, POP'

"Ugh," Slim grunted.

'POP, POP, POP, POP, POP'

There were a series of shots but when the smoke cleared the shooter was dead and Honestii was holding the smoking gun.

"Come on baby, we gotta go!" I shouted trying to wiggle Nahmir up off me. I could barely breathe due to the gunshot wound to my left thigh.

"Oh my God!" Honestii shouted as she rushed over and rolled Nahmir off me. "He's shot!"

"Is he breathing?" I panicked.

"Yes, he has a pulse," Honestii stated calmly as she pulled me to my feet. "We have to get him to the car, and we can't carry him."

"What are we gonna do?" I cried just thinking about my man dying. I couldn't lose him. I just couldn't.

"We're gonna have to drag him Sis. That's the only way we're gonna get out of here without getting caught up."

Honestii grabbed one of his arms and I held on to the other. It hurt like hell to limp on my leg, but I didn't give a damn. I had to save Nahmir.

"We gotta get you outta here!"

"I gotta get this phone out!" I thought as I dug Ruga's cell out and tossed it on the floor in plain view.

"Good thinking Sis!" Honestii panted as we continued to drag my man out of the house.

"Ugh!" He grunted as soon as we hit the graveled road.

"Oh shit, baby you okay? We're gonna get you some help!"

"Nah, just get us out of here!" He insisted as we got him to the car and lifted him in the backseat.

I got back there with him while Honestii hopped into the driver's seat and peeled off. That was when we heard the sirens approaching. It was too late though. We were already hitting the back road that led directly to the freeway.

"Where's the nearest hospital?" My sister panicked as she veered onto the highway heading west.

"No fucking hospital!" Nahmir yelled as he struggled to unzip his jacket and showed us that he was wearing a bullet proof vest.

"Fucker you had me scared!" I shouted while punching him in the arm. "That shit ain't cool!"

"Hush and come here baby," he insisted as he pulled me into his arms. "I love you."

"Huh?" I asked just to have him repeat it.

"I love you," he confessed once again before laying a deep kiss on me. When he released me, I stare into his eyes? This time I knew that it was sincere.

"What?" He asked.

"Nothing..."

"No, what is it Khouri?" He pried with concern.

"It's nothing. I just wanted to tell you that I told you so..." I teased with a peck to his lips.

"You told me what?" He asked not quite understanding me.

I just giggled, because the only thing that was important is that he had said it, and I wasn't gonna lose him.

"It's nothing, I promise."

"I hope you know that I have always loved you, girl."

"You have?" I cried.

"Aw you have?" Honestii chimed in.

"Hush Sissy," I cried even harder.

"Yes, and I'm gonna show you just how much as soon as we get back and count this money."

I heard my sister giggling as she veered off on the exit. She makes me sick.

Nahmir and I both just laughed. It was funny how things had a way of working out...

Honestii called Marlon and told him briefly what happened as soon as they got home. They needed help because Khouri was still bleeding from the bullet to her thigh. She needed it removed.

Marlon immediately instructed Honestii to drive her sister to the East Side Clinic that was about ten minutes away from where they were. Although it was after hours, he had his good friend meet them over there.

Luckily there was no major damage done to Khouri. Dr. Brice Boxley was able to remove the bullet from her leg in no time then patched her up good.

Nahmir and the two sisters stayed there until the next day. That was when Marlon showed up and took them all to his house out by the mountains.

That's was where all them stayed for the next few weeks. In pure seclusion; four million dollars richer...

"It's about time I get back to the office. I done used up all my vacation days, sick days and personal leave," Marlon stated as he joined everyone in the family room. "You guys ready to go back to the city?"

"I know I am," Honestii replied while staring closely at the television becoming completely distracted. "You guys see this?"

My sister shooed Nahmir up off her and rushed to the television to turn up the volume.

Morning news*: Lenard Stevens on the streets known as 'Ruga' was found dead today. He was shot in his home, assassination style. It was discovered that it was in connection with the drug deal that went bad earlier this month when four people were murdered, included a young pregnant woman... The money was never recovered...*

The words traveled off in the air as Khouri sat in front of the television with her mouth wide open. "Damn, Paula was pregnant?" She couldn't believe it...None of them could.

It had been a whole week since they had even turned on the news. They all had been avoiding it because they didn't want to worry about the outside world. The only reason they had to was because they were heading back home, and they wanted to know what they were walking into.

"Damn," Honestii repeated.

"Damn is right!" Marlon snapped. "I hope everyone learned a valuable lesson from all this?"

Honestii turned her head and thought about her little secret that she was holding. She hadn't told Marlon or her sister. She was still waiting for the right moment.

"Yeah, I'm sorry I even got you guys into this shit. It was me that was always pressing you two to do more and more. Now that I see how close I was to losing you Khouri, I regret that shit. I'm sorry baby."

Khouri ran over to Nahmir and fell into his arms. They hugged momentarily before Marlon interrupted.

"Well, Khouri, Honestii? Y'all ain't got shit to say?" Marlon asked.

Khouri was the next one to speak up.

"Yes, I have something to say about all the events that led us to this point. I haven't been able to think of anything else to be honest. I should have listened to my little sister and stopped it after Mama was killed! I didn't though! I was greedy and only thought about myself! Look, now our cousin is dead and Ruga is too! Hell yeah, I learned! I will never steal again and if I need revenge, next time I'll wait for that Bytch Named Karma!"

Breaking down in tears, Khouri placed her face in her hands.

"What about you Honestii?" Marlon focused all his attention on his fiancée.

Without saying a word, she went to the home pregnancy test she had taken earlier. It was positive.

"Here, this is to show you I'm done!" Honestii smiled as she revealed her good news. "I damn sho' ain't bringing my baby up in this shit! Yes, I learned my lesson!"

Marlon broke down in tears over the happy news.

"I can't wait to be a father."

"I can't wait to be a mother and your wife baby," Honestii replied.

"That's beautiful," Nahmir spoke.

"Yes, I'm so happy for them."

"You'll be next if I have anything to do with it, baby," Nahmir told her.

"Not in this lifetime baby," Khouri replied.

Not only was she richer, but she had rights to everything that belonged to Ruga. Her life was about to be set. A kid was the last thing on her mind...

The End

CPSIA information can be obtained
at www.ICGtesting.com
Printed in the USA
LVHW031929100220
646421LV00014B/973